TAKEN BY THE HITMAN

ALEXIS ABBOTT

Get an EXCLUSIVE book, **FREE** just as a thank you for signing up for my newsletter! Plus you'll never miss a new release, cover reveal, or promotion!

http://alexisabbott.com/newsletter

KONSTANTIN

Snow as pristine as the first day of winter falls softly from the cloudy skies, never knowing how cruelly it mocks those of us slowly freezing to death in the prison yard of Krasnoyarsk.

Guards patrol the high stone walls lined with barbed wire, and all we can see on the far, forested hills over the tops of those oppressive borders is the occasional light or plume of smoke from a house. Some of my fellow inmates make a pastime of making up stories about their residents. I've joined them, once or twice. We suppose the little red house to the northeast houses a lovely young woman who has to tend to the few farm animals she has left after her father fell too ill to work. We suppose the white house to the northeast has a young woodsman in it who will one day come lend a hand, but we've seen little traffic on those remote roads so far this winter.

Today, though, I don't join them in supposing anything. My mind is too preoccupied with the very present reality of what I've been offered this morning, in a place where being offered anything is more scarce than daylight in this icy, derelict place.

The guards exercise us in the yard. Lined up in formation, we are put through routine exercises that keep the blood flowing, all of us outfitted in heavy uniform jackets that do little to keep out the biting cold. To the seasoned veterans who might die behind these walls, this has become as routine as breathing. They go through every exercise without even needing the guards' commands, and sometimes, I wonder whether they'll keep doing them at the same times if they're released into the free world once again. I wonder if this place will ever truly leave any of them.

The newly enslaved inmates are harder to watch. Many of them are young men in prison for crimes of necessity — for thievery, for fighting back, for leading the criminal lives the law and poverty forced them into. Many of them still have the spark of life burning in their eyes. The same spark that I feel fading from mine with every passing day. They shiver as they fumble through their exercises, glancing from side to side and wondering if this nightmare is as real as it feels.

I call them 'enslaved,' for that is what it means to be in prison. We eat on command, we sleep on command, we piss on command, and we toil for no wages on command. The state finds in us a source of legal slavery in an institution that is worldwide. And if there is one passion that has not faded but grown stronger in these months in prison, it is my hatred for slavery.

Our exercises conclude and we're given a few minutes of imaginary freedom to wander the yard and talk. Though I must admit, such a regulated life looks a lot like my life in the Spetznaz — the Russian elite Special Forces — did. And if I agree to carry out what I've been tasked with, my life here will end every bit as bloodily as my life in the military did.

I move over to a planter and have a seat nearby a group of older men who are playing cards, blending in with the three other burly men watching the game. Nobody says anything, and I suspect the old men didn't say anything to each other when they got the game started. They didn't need to.

My eyes want to drift to a certain person on the opposite end of the yard, but I force them to fall in line and obey my self-control. I cannot be seen observing him, watching his every move as I wrestle with whether I will carry out what has been asked of me.

I ask myself whether I will kill my target.

The Bratva presence in prison is strong. The eight-pointed star that marks their members is visible on their chests, backs, and arms in the shower, and other prisoners are quick to point them out to new inmates who get funny ideas about starting fights. I was never one to engage in such petty things. When I arrived in prison, I had every intention of living out a quiet sentence in my cell, burning through books that I'd often heard of but never thought to read. That would be the only distraction from the burning thorn of slavery in my side, a thorn I knew I'd never again be able to extract from others as long as I was in shackles. But it seems that upon my arrival, word spread quickly about the nature of my crime. I wondered who among the guards spilled the story of what had me removed from the Spetznaz, since I'd hardly spoken to anyone behind these bars, but I suspected it could be any one of them. Some of them must be truly curious as to why I was spared execution for treason.

Whatever the case, my plans for a quiet life were dashed to the ground this morning. I'd been visited by a man I didn't recognize, yet he'd introduced himself as a loving uncle. He gave me his warmest regards, wished me the best for my sentence, and given me a thick book that the guards suspiciously did not check when I brought it back to my cell.

Inside the hollowed-out book was a note bearing a name and an eight-pointed red star, and it was wrapped around a shank.

The message was clear. This man was to die, and I would gain the favor of the Bratva. But I did not act immediately. I may be a slave, but I am no dog to bite on his faceless master's orders. So I did some probing around about this Iosif Ivanovic that I was asked to kill, partly because I knew him to be one of the men bearing a red star on his chest.

Eavesdropping on the whispering of other made men of the Bratva accomplished what I needed.

"Did you drop the payload in the-"

"Quiet. Ivanovic has rats in the walls."

I kept an eye on him during breakfast and lunch to confirm what this suggested. Indeed, around the man, there always seemed to be a guard within earshot. When he got up and passed through the sea of other inmates, running a hand through his greasy gray hair and snorting, a guard chose this time to make his rounds in that section. When we were marched into the exercise grounds, he had a guard beside him when he passed by prisoners from other cell blocks.

He was protected. Protected against someone like me. He was a rat.

Contempt could have easily grown in my heart for him. Those who chose to stick their heads up the asses of our oppressive masters were just as bad as the masters themselves, if not worse. It is no wonder he is disliked, either. He's been in this place for a relatively short sentence, but he has luxuries that none of the older inmates have, and he lords it over them. He's started to gain a following, a few other younger inmates clinging to him for safety, the one glimmer of warmth in this cold place. To that end, I feel almost bad at the thought of slaying him, but I know that their simpering is a short-term solution to their pain. They've turned their backs on solidarity.

They've turned their backs on the Bratva.

Iosif and his small entourage sit on the far end of the yard, and even now, there are two or three of the newer inmates sitting around him as he speaks to them like a teacher explaining things. Now I see why the Bratva wants him dead sooner rather than later, and perhaps why they're interested in someone like me doing the deed. If he's allowed to go on much longer, he'll have a small army of spies doing his bidding in the prison, and by extension, the bidding of the guards. I only afford myself one glance at him to size up the men around him before I look back to the card game in front of me. Men like Iosif are paranoid beyond reason.

A bell rings, and the barks of the guards indicate that we're to head back inside. Within seconds, we all fall into line, and the guards to a quick headcount of us all. As everyone is accounted for, I notice one of the guards moving Iosif aside, to his confusion. I can't help but glance over to him, but I grimace faintly as I realize he's being moved with the high-security prisoners, those who've done deadly crimes and require special attention.

I had planned to follow him back to his bunk and do the deed there, but I know now that's not an option. Someone must have tipped the guards off. All the more reason to make this job quick and quiet.

I don't know what it is that's made me suddenly so willing to carry this deed out. Maybe it's the drive to protect my fellow slaves from those who would prey upon them from within and without. My thoughts flit back to my childhood on the streets of Moscow, and I see in these other men the faces of the boys I grew up with. Us against the world. Slaves to circumstance.

Or maybe I was just born to be a killer. A hitman.

I march with the rest of the men back to my bed, one of many lined up in a long, wide, open room. There is no privacy here. As I sit down on my bed and the guards patrol past, I feel the book that I've hidden within my mattress. It feels particularly hard beneath me, a burning presence, reminding me of what is to come. I cannot take it out now. Not when so many people are still looking about them, many of them fresh and wide-eyed.

Across the room, Iosif's bed is getting assigned to one of the new inmates. I frown, my suspicions confirmed. He's being moved to a place with higher security. It's a risk on their part; arousing suspicion about Iosif, even to protect him, jeopardizes his position as an informant. And of course, being out of the general public means that he has less influence. I imagine he'll be moved back within a few weeks.

I don't want to wait a few weeks.

One thing clues me into where he is, though. I notice two of the men I know to be loyal to him whispering to each other, and after a few moments, they get up and head out of the room, in the direction of the bathrooms.

Iosif never uses the bathroom alone. It's one of the few places where he's lightly guarded, so he keeps his own men around him. He'll probably be meeting with them there before getting moved. My window of opportunity just shrank.

Glancing about, I take out my book, shoving it under the covers and transferring the shank to my pants before taking it out and pretending to find my place in it again. After a few moments, once I'm sure nobody's looking, I replace the empty book under my mattress. I need a distraction. In a room full of testosterone-fueled men, this isn't a difficult task.

The man on the bunk next to mine is glaring across the room at another man. I'd seen them blowing up at each other briefly in the yard yesterday before the guards intervened. They were former accomplices of some kind. As I get up to go use the bathroom, I whisper something in his ear about what the other man said about him during exercise today, and that's all it takes to have him getting up and crossing the room. By the time I'm out into the hall, the sounds of a fight are already breaking out, and the guard who had been about to follow me gets distracted, rushing into the bunk room to break up the two men.

I have to move quickly. I pass the stone walls of the facility until the restroom comes into view. Everyone knows it's Iosif's bathroom, and there's a guard posted at the front, as always. Sometimes it's a surprise he even needs protection, with all the attention offered him by the guards.

What happens next, I know will cost me dearly. But life in a hopeless cell will push a man to drastic limits. The guard gives me a meaningful glance as I start to walk by. My hands are too quick, though, when I turn and deliver a hard, precise strike to the side of his head, and he crumples to the ground, cold.

There are cameras in the facility. No matter what happens next, I'm going to spend the rest of my time here in maximum security after this, if the guards don't kill me. With purpose, I stride into the bathroom.

I hear a conversation taking place within, and the sound of my footsteps gives them pause. They aren't used to being interrupted. I turn a corner, and the two men who'd left the bunk room are lounging by the sinks, and there's one closed stall in the bathroom.

"What fucking guard let you in? You're in the

wrong bathroo-" one starts to say before my fist connects with his head. The element of surprise gone, his friend shouts for a guard and lunges for me. I sidestep him easily, bringing my knee up to his gut and pounding my elbow into his spine as he goes down with a shout. To my surprise he gets up again, scrambling for my legs, but I catch him by the collar and lift him with one arm, slamming him into the sink. Teeth clatter to the ground as he slumps, unconscious, and I step calmly to the closed stall door.

With one solid kick, I force the door open, and it swings aside, revealing my target, sitting on the toilet with his pants around his ankles, his beady eyes focused on me. He knows when he's been gotten.

"I was wondering when they'd send someone after me," he says, his voice a smoker's rasp. "But to send you, of all people? An insult."

I step forward, my face stony. His scraggly-bearded face is twisted into a sneer as he watches me approach, and I draw the shank out of my pants.

"You judge me, I see it in your eyes," he says with a mirthless laugh. "But how can you? We're both traitors, you and I. Do you not see the irony in their actions, sending a traitor after a traitor? You're disposable to them. They will turn on you. And one day, you'll find some young buck catching you with your pants down."

Without a word, I reach down to his prison uniform, tearing the shirt apart and exposing that red star on his chest, and I drive my shank deep into it, straight to his twisted heart as he grips my hands in vain.

His grip starts to slacken, the grimace on his face fading as blood starts to pour from his chest, and I feel the boot of a guard kicking into the back of my leg, and the nightstick blows start to rain down on me.

I don't know how much time passes while I'm unconscious. When I start to awaken in the hospital wing, the slow drip of anesthetic soothing my nerves, I see one of the nurses leaning over my chest, poking something in. I fight to stay awake, raising my hand a little through the sedatives. Maybe Iosif was right. Maybe I'd done my part, and they'd sent someone in to finish me off.

But as the man leaning over me brushes my hand away, he stands up, and I look down to see the fresh marks of the red, eight-pointed star he is tattooing over my heart.

"Wake up, Rosie, wake up!" squeaks the high-pitched voice from one side of my rickety little futon in the living room. I'm already awake, and have been for probably hours, just lying here protesting the early morning hours, hoping in vain that I might fall back asleep. I should know better by now. My body knows when to get up, like clockwork. As soon as the girls open their eyes in the morning, it's like a magical internal alarm clock starts chirping in my head. It comes from years and years of being the one who awoke with their cries in the middle of the night to soothe them and rock them back to silent contentment.

I've been a mother to these girls, my little sisters, for their entire lives — a long, exhausting eight years so far. The twins have me wrapped around their little fingers, and they hang on my every word and look. After all, eight years of adversity will do that to you, bring people together in a way good times never really can. We've always been here for each other, because nobody else will have our backs if we don't.

But today I have absolutely no desire to get out of the thrift-store futon I call a bed, because today marks a darkly momentous occasion: my eighteenth birthday.

On television, there are so many young women looking forward to this milestone, longing for freedom and maturity in a way I'll never really comprehend. But maybe it's just because for all these years I've gotten all the maturity and freedom I could ever want for a whole lifetime. Not that freedom means much when you have two tiny twin sisters who need to be fed, bathed, clothed, entertained, and looked after. When Daisy and Sunny were just babies and I was barely more than a child myself, there were dark times when I considered taking them to a church or fire station and just leaving them there. Not for lack of love, of course, but because I simply thought they would be better off with someone else, someone older with more time, money, and experience than me.

It's been a grueling, uphill battle, trying to keep all my ducks in a row all this time. And it's not like my good-for-nothing, gambling boozer of a father has done anything to make our lives easier. He's our legal guardian, naturally, as the state somehow still sees him as fit for fatherhood. But Frank Barnes is little more than an occasional visitor who blunders around our tiny, shotgun-style house in a drunken rage, bellowing obscenities and chucking whatever heavy object is closest at me. The one saving grace I can thank God for is the fact that for the most part, my father's violence is generally only targeted at me. I'm bigger and stronger than the little ones, so if one of us is going to have to bear the torture, I am relieved to have it be me rather than either of them.

And I know why he hates me more than them… It's because I look the most like him, and he absolutely despises himself. I am sure he knows deep down how much of a sorry loser he really is, and it's eating him up inside just as much as the alcohol and endless debts are.

Daisy climbs onto the futon to straddle me and bat me gently with a patched-up throw pillow while Sunny pokes my arm repeatedly, both of them giggling. I have to summon every ounce of self-control not to let my mouth break into a grin, but I'm committed to my Sleeping Beauty act. I know the longer I stay asleep, the more frustrated and ridiculous my sisters will get, and I can't resist working them into a mini-frenzy trying to get me out of bed.

"Rosie! It's morning!" Sunny whispers plaintively,

slumping her pointed little chin onto my shoulder. "You have to get up! I'm hungry."

"And it's your birthday," Daisy adds brightly, trying to entice me out of bed. She wouldn't understand that my birthday is exactly the reason I *don't* want to get up.

It's yet another reminder of how off-course my life has gotten. I graduated high school a couple weeks ago in May, after transferring halfway through my senior year from down South. Originally, we are all from Mississippi, a tiny town near Biloxi. But my dad's gambling debts got him into hot water and he forced us all to climb into our piece of shit grey van and move up here to New Jersey.

Of course, instead of realizing that maybe, just maybe, his gambling problem has become too much for anyone to handle... he simply moved us right into another little town near a casino hotspot. We're within thirty minutes of Atlantic City. Typical. I don't know if he's just stupid, or if he really, truly just doesn't care anymore. I suppose it's probably some of both.

He's always been prone to rash decision-making, but ever since Mama died, what was formerly just a lovable personality quirk has blossomed into a fully-grown, crippling issue. It wasn't always this bad, though. When I was a little girl, I was pretty happy, believe it or not. Granted, we never had much money or anything, but we lived a fairly good life down in Mississippi. I was young enough to be oblivious to my parents' problems with money and alcohol, especially since I spent the majority of my time running around through the marshy woods, playing barefoot and free surrounded by nature. I was always a bit of a loner, preferring to make up stories and have adventures with my imaginary friends rather than mingle with the other kids in our trailer park. Besides, most of them only wanted to sit around and watch TV, try to sneak money and cigarettes from their moms' purses.

And even though we lived in a trailer, my mom always did her very best to make it feel like a real home, decorating it with bright colors and aromatic flowers and herbs. We had a lovely garden out back, where she grew tomatoes and thyme, teaching me how to take a seed and nurture it into a successful bloom. I think she is the one who taught me patience and compassion, who showed me how to be kind and quiet when life required it. If not for her, I don't think I could have managed taking care of Daisy and Sunny all these years.

And even my father was a better man back then. My mom, Susanna, kept him in high spirits with her constant singing and laughter. She sounded just like Judy Garland when she sang, and even her laugh was lightly musical. I remember her always dressed in colorful, heavily-patterned dresses she stitched together from rummage sale fabrics. Even though it might have looked garish or costume-like on someone else, my mother always managed to pull it off perfectly. Perhaps because it suited her personality so well. She was a ray of sunshine, making the best out of even the darkest situations. She knew how to repurpose everything, how to turn a dud into a dream without fail.

Ever since she died, it's like even the sun can't muster the same quality of light anymore.

I was ten years old when she passed away, just a little girl playing with a knock-off Barbie doll in the hospital waiting room while my dad paced back and forth. We were awaiting the long delayed births of my little sisters, and up until the very day they were born, the doctors were certain that all was well. But when my mother kept bleeding hours and hours after the twins emerged screaming and kicking, it became quickly evident that there was something very, very wrong.

My mother died that same day, while the newborns slept in their identical pink blankets down the hall and my father fell to his knees, the wind utterly stolen from his lungs, the light swept straight out of his life. I didn't understand it at first — how we could all go from blissful and excited to totally devastated. It didn't make any sense to me. Just twenty-four hours before, I had been sitting beside my mom's hospital bed playing go-fish with a deck of cards, both of us laughing while the doctors ticked things down in their charts. How could she be so full of life one moment, and then completely still and empty the next?

When the doctors explained that my mother was gone, I heard the horrified, blood-churning wail my father let out, from all the way down the hall. I dropped my Barbie and looked up instantly, unable to process that the sound had come from my strong, silent father. He came stumbling through the lobby with a glazed, wide-eyed look on his face, as though he were incapable of deciding on an appropriate facial expression for the circumstances. He didn't respond to my questions, totally ignoring me.

It was the first time he pushed me down, shoving me aside onto the sterile hospital tile like I was nothing. But even worse still was the way he fully neglected the twins. He wanted nothing to do with them, blaming them for his wife's death. It didn't help that they were born with full heads of tufty blonde hair — barely hours old and already resembling their mother. I, on the other hand, have always been pale with dark hair like my father.

A nurse came out to quietly ask what he wanted to name his new daughters, and he waved his hand to dismiss her, like he couldn't care less. I piped up and said, "Daddy, you have to name them or they're… they're not real."

I remember still, as clearly as though it happened yesterday, the way his dark blue eyes so similar to mine landed on me, cold and steely. Totally unfeeling. He said, "You name them. I don't care."

At first, the nurse had tried to protest, but I quickly jumped in to intervene. Even then, as a ten-year-old child, I knew better than to try and reason with my father when he was angry. It was the turning point. From that moment on, something monumental had shifted in my world. My mother's light no longer lit the dark shadows of our impoverished little existence. I aged a million years in one instant, turning to the nurse and giving her the first two names I could think of: Daisy and Sunny. Because it was a beautiful summer's day, almost too beautiful to contain such a horrible outcome.

Thinking back now wryly, I realize how fitting it is in many ways. I, for one, was named Rosalie after my dad's favorite Thin Lizzy song. He says it was the song stuck in his head the whole time my mom was in labor with me, so it was fate. (I'd say it was probably more like a coincidence than an act of God, but here we are.) And my mom would have loved the twins' names, as she was always growing things and singing in the sunshine. But it was like the moment I gave them their names, I became their protector. From that moment onward, they were mine. My babies.

For a while, a nurse came to visit us and help us — well, me — learn how to feed, bathe, and change the twins' diapers. I caught on quickly, knowing that if I didn't, nobody would. My father was a different man already, going out on days-long benders and coming home only to sit catatonic at the window as though expecting my mom to come flouncing down the little pathway as she always did.

I was grieving, too, of course. But I simply didn't have the time or luxury of letting my heartbreak paralyze me like my father. I had to raise two tiny little girls, essentially by myself.

"Let's pour cold water on her," Daisy suggests, jerking me back to the present moment.

"No, let's tickle her!" Sunny insists.

Neither one of those options is one I plan on entertaining, so I finally, begrudgingly, open my eyes and immediately capture both girls in my arms with an animalistic growl. They shriek in delighted laughter, folding into my chest happily.

"You have awakened the beast!" I hiss, pretending to gnaw on Sunny's hands like an animal. She recoils with a squeal.

"It's the beast's birthday!" Daisy brings up, yet again. I want so badly to just tell her not to talk about it, to let it go. But I can't dampen her spirits that way. There are so few reasons for us to celebrate, ever, and I don't want to take this away from her so harshly.

"Yep, and I think I need a bowl of cereal to get me started," I say, moving them both aside so I can get up and stretch. The twins exchange nervous looks.

"Um, there isn't any cereal left," Sunny admits in a tiny, timid voice.

"We had it for dinner last night, remember?" Daisy quips, fidgeting.

My heart sinks, remembering how we perused the whole kitchen in desperation, hoping to find something edible to quell their growling stomachs. The ache in my own belly reminds me that I skipped dinner altogether last night so that they could eat.

There's no food in the house.

Yet again.

This is why, instead of preparing for college like most of my fellow high school graduates, I have been trolling through the help wanted ads in the paper for a job. I need some kind of revenue coming into this household that doesn't simply slither right back out the window and into a slot machine. Dad works long hours at a pawn shop, but the only thing he really spends his money on are trips to the casinos. When we were younger, on the rare occasion that he actually won a little bit of money, he would spontaneously take us out of school and go out for a fancy dinner and night of bowling or a movie. But nowadays, even when he did win, the money just funneled right back onto a blackjack table.

He doesn't even pretend to care anymore, only coming home to sleep or to make my life a living hell with his rage tantrums and violent outbursts. I want to hate him, and on the surface level, perhaps I do.

But deep down, I will always love my father, because I can't help but recall the fond memories I have of him from when I was a little girl. When things were still good.

"Well, I think I have a little bit of money in the piggy bank," I say suddenly, remembering the fifteen or sixteen dollars of cash I still have left from the waitressing job I had last summer. "How do we feel about going to the waffle place down the street?"

The girls immediately jump to their feet and rush to hug me enthusiastically, both of them murmuring their thanks. It breaks my heart that something so simple could make them so happy. I want to give them so much more, show them a better life. I want them to be happier than I am.

But that's hard to do all by myself.

Just as we are finally dressed and ready to walk out the door, my father's van comes wobbling up the driveway. My stomach flip-flops, anxiety settling into my veins instantly. Out of a natural protective instinct, I pull the girls in close, an arm around each of them. I stand tall, my chin tilted slightly upward to show my defiance. I have learned how to stand my ground when I need to.

Frank Barnes all but spills out of the driver's seat, clearly already at least half a sheet to the wind even though it's barely nine in the morning. Alcoholism has no clock.

I half-expect him to lumber over and take a

swing at me, but instead he simply gives us a wide smile and says, "Happy birthday, kiddo. Got you a big surprise."

I regard him warily, not trusting him. I have no idea what this could mean. My dad is pretty unpredictable these days, and I cannot remember the last time he gave me any kind of birthday gift.

He straightens up and says, "We're going on a little boat ride, you and me. The girls will be alright here at home for the day, won't they?" He addresses the last question in a higher pitch, looking at Daisy and Sunny, who only nod reluctantly. They know better than to question or defy him, even when he's in a somewhat good mood. The least little thing can set him off.

So, even though I don't want to leave them behind, I have no choice but to obey and climb into the passenger seat of the van, without a clue where the hell we were going.

I look out the plane window to see the Statue of Liberty standing in the water, and I raise my eyebrows. She's smaller than I imagined her.

"New York City," says Anton Budurov, the man who twelve hours ago I thought was going to try to kill me. "It's even more overwhelming from the ground level, I promise you that. And Konstantin, we run this city. You're going to be a part of something truly beautiful here."

I boarded this private jet back in Moscow at Anton's request. He's a higher-up in the Bratva, and someone I've taken jobs from on more than one occasion in my ten years of service, and when such a man makes a request, it's generally more of an order. At least, that would be true of most men serving the Bratva. It's been a long time since prison, a decade, and I have come a long way from suffering to take blind orders from notes in hollowed-out books. Now, I'm a man of contracts, but this hasn't slowed my rise through the ranks of our association.

Nonetheless, a plane ride alone with a man of Anton's rank could mean any number of things. So I could not have been more surprised when he informed me that I was being sent to America.

"This place isn't what it was ten years ago, Konstantin," he says, still in our native Russian, swirling his brandy in his glass while eyeing the city in the midday sun. "It is not at all like Russia. A new beast entirely." He raises an eyebrow at me with a smile. "All those vices you're so fond of butting heads with in Russia? This is where the demand funnels it all. America." He smiles, and it turns into a laugh, while all I afford him is a light nod.

"I know what you're thinking," Anton says with a smile, wagging his finger at me. "You're wondering how all this bluster and speech tells you why a hitman's services are required by us here. Well, my friend, there are two answers to this. One, there is *always* need of a hitman in New York. Two," he flashes a grin at me, "you aren't being brought here to be a hitman."

I raise my eyebrows at this news. Anton is not the kind of man to beat around the bush, generally, his balding head, square face, and sharp eyes always direct and to the point. It bodes ill when such men speak cryptically.

"No?" I ask.

"No," he affirms, laughing at my reticence. "Of course, we aren't exactly going to New York City proper. You're going to a place where most of us Russians congregate, where our grandfathers' fathers first put down the roots that would give birth to our Bratva in the US."

"Brighton Beach," I say, hardly surprised. It was the hub of Russian activity in the NYC area.

"Yes, my friend," he says, grinning, "a corner of the state brimming with opportunity." Despite Anton's candor, the declaration sits uneasily with me.

I have something of a reputation in the Bratva. I have long known that they have been the facilitators of the notorious human trafficking market in and out of New York City, a vicious trade that buys and sells the flesh of nubile young women for their horrendous buyers' darkest whims. I have stood against such inhumanity since before my induction to the Bratva. Before even my imprisonment. So when I was brought on as a hired killer, and even now as I work for contracts, my colleagues keep a watchful eye on everything I do. I think this rather silly. My skill is of no question, and I have slain men with such deadly precision that even those made men who rank far above me hear my name and respect what it means. But for me to oppose the slave trade that has brought in so much money for the Bratva? This, they say, is playing a game far over my head, and many of the enemies I've attracted over the years have tested me, but my enemies have learned that to do so is to goad death like a bull-fighter.

This is why they call me the Bull.

So when men like Anton, who stand close enough to my position to claw his way over me on his path to the top, seem so openly elated, it puts a sour taste in my mouth.

But I know he'll only keep talking in circles if I don't humor him. "And what opportunity is there so great that you drag me out of the Motherland for it, Anton?" Some rivals to deal with, I have no doubt. Anton is a man to keep his friends close and his enemies closer, and as long as I am both, I could be the perfect weapon in his hands while I'm here.

"For you, my friend?" he says as a flight attendant comes by with another tray of drinks, and Anton takes a glass for himself. "Let me tell you. Sergei Slokavich. You know his name, do you not?"

Now my eyebrows furrow, and I know I'm being challenged. Sergei was a Bratva kingpin in the Brighton area for years. He was also the leader of one of the biggest sex slavery rings the Bratva has ever boasted, and it raked him in so much money that he could afford to ship his bastard son over to live with him in luxury, wine, and women. Until recently, at least.

"I know he is dead," I say firmly, looking Anton in the eye, "killed by someone from within. How could I have not heard? You're toying around a point, Anton."

"Indeed he is," Anton says, grinning piggishly at me. "He and his spoiled brat of a son, along with his legacy, dead and thoroughly smeared. And there's a bit of a power vacuum in his place. Brighton Beach is not the most stable locale in the country, for all its potential."

I frown, sitting back. "So I'm to be your sword as you fight your way to the top, is that it?" I say, crossing my legs. "You of all people should know that there will be no shortage of contracts that I'll be willing to take here, Anton. I won't be playing bodyguard and murder for you around the clock."

"Konstantin!" he cries, holding his heart and feigning a dramatic strain. "Konstantin, my boy, you do me such a disservice! To think I'd abuse you so! Shame on you for being so rude, especially to the man who's giving you news of your new promotion."

I blink, not certain I'd heard Anton correctly, but as he grins proudly at my surprise, I realize that he isn't joking, and I can't help but look dumbfounded.

"That's right, my friend," he says, sticking his hand out for me to shake, "you're not accompanying me to America — I'm escorting you, the new head of operations here in Brighton Beach."

I extend my hand to meet his, hardly able to believe what I'm hearing. "Me, replacing Slokavich?" I repeat. "I'm being made the *pakhan* of Brighton Beach?" I feel a small smile tugging at my face to match Anton's jolly laughter, and he nods, patting my hand.

"Just so, Anton, just so — or I suppose I should be calling you *boss* now, eh?"

The news is almost dizzying. I knew that I was respected among the mafia, and it's true that I've been climbing the ranks so quickly that some might call me ambitious. But the more I think of the circumstances, the more it makes sense, to my surprise.

"Konstantin, as one of the men involved in this decision, I can say wholeheartedly that this is a long time coming" he goes on, leaning back in his chair and looking out the window fondly at the city. "You've been our most capable man in Moscow since I first scouted you in the prison and paid your way out. You've been responsible for some of the grandest power plays the Bratva in Russia has ever seen. But don't think your powers of leadership have gone unnoticed," he says, and I can't help but notice how heavily he's laying on the compliments. This explains the lavish private jet and the friendly treatment, I think to myself.

"Brighton Beach's men are in a position to make a lot of changes in the next few months," he says, taking on a more serious tone. "Power has shifted rapidly, and while Brighton is a thoroughly Russian haven, we cannot limit ourselves to that corner of the metropolis alone. There is much more up for grabs, and much more to be wrestled from the other mobs out there."

I lean forward, steepling my hands. "So the movers and shakers in NYC have their eyes on who, the Irish? The Italians?"

"All that and more is yet to be seen," he says, taking a long swig of his drink. "And many of those choices will be up to you, Konstantin. All I know is that we need someone capable running the show if we're to keep from getting cornered in the city. A weak *pakhan* in Brighton could mean the next mob over gets ambitious, and then you've got a great pile of bullshit on your plate," he says, waving a hand dismissively.

I nod, feeling my ears pop as we start to descend even further, the jet making its way to the airport. As we descend, I can't help but think about what this new power structure is going to mean for my business. Power structure or no, I am and always will be a contract killer. I am swift, I am silent, and I strike with precision. I have no doubts that I can run a small city's Bratva. But that part of New York is a beast bread on deep-seated corruption of precisely the type I've stood against in all my time as a made man.

And now, to find myself with a position of authority thrust upon me in the middle of what is certain to be a tremendous shift in power? Something in the back of my mind tells me that I'm being set up for a fight. That I'm being tossed into a pit of fresh, ambitious enemies ready to come at me from all sides while I get my bearings.

Another part of me welcomes that challenge.

"We'll worry about the business side of things tomorrow, though," Anton interrupts my thoughts, tapping the window and pointing down towards the harbor. "You have the kinds of accommodations you can imagine for a man of your stature. We have a penthouse on the upscale side of town ready for you now, and you'll be able to stay there tonight, if you can find your way to a taxi. And I'll be surprised if you can, considering the little get-together the others have planned for you. See that ship? Five docks down from the bottom edge there, the one with the blue flags along the sides. That's our yacht for tonight."

"Our yacht?" I repeat, raising an eyebrow.

"Indeed," he says with a grin. "Because, my friend, your new associates are going to want to meet you. After all, what is a promotion without a celebration?"

As my dad yanks the van into reverse and starts backing out onto the street, I watch Daisy and Sunny get smaller and smaller, their freckly faces morose and concerned. It makes my heart ache to see such grown-up fear and weariness on such young faces. Their eyes are wide and honey-brown like our mother's, but right now every fleck of color looks to have been dip-dyed in sadness. I have to fight the urge to kick the passenger door open and jump out of the moving van, run back to my girls and wrap them in a big hug.

I don't know where my father is taking me, but some small echo of intuition in my brain gives me a sense of finality. Like this is the end of one thing, and the beginning of something else. Suddenly, I am filled with urgency, like I need to go back and memorize Daisy and Sunny's faces, hold them in my arms and imprint their warmth on my soul, just in case I never get another chance.

But that's silly, right? Chaotic, catastrophic thinking?

Surely I will see them again. This is probably just some half-baked attempt on my father's part to bond with me or whatever. As if he's ever done anything to deserve a bond with me in the past eight years, anyway. In fact, I reason with myself, it's more likely that he just wants me to take part in a scam of some kind. One of my dad's rarely successful and never legal get-fast-quick schemes he comes up with while he's drunk off his ass.

Or maybe, since it's my birthday, he's just going to use me to score free drinks at some seedy little bar. Especially since a lot of the bars he frequents could not care less about the legal drinking age. I'm only eighteen, not twenty-one, but as much business as these bars get from my father, they'll certainly make an exception. Hell, my dad probably keeps most of these places in business single-handedly, his alcoholism is so intense.

"Dad, where are we going?" I ask finally, breaking the silence. He grins, the faint traces of a once-handsome face appearing momentarily. Once in a blue moon, when a particularly good mood strikes him, he can almost be mistaken for the same charismatic man he once was long ago. But today, I know better than to trust his smile. The father I knew and loved is long gone, buried under years of wandering lost. My mother is the one who died, but in reality I lost both of my parents that fateful day.

"Well, if I tell ya, it won't be a surprise, would it?" he replies teasingly, stealing a sidelong glance at me as he plows through a four-way stop without even acknowledging the stop sign. A woman in a Volkswagen bug honks at us and my dad flips her the bird, the grin never leaving his face.

I am fairly accustomed to my father's horrifying driving habits, after years of riding shotgun in this death trap. As far as Frank Barnes is concerned, traffic laws are really just loose guidelines only losers and sober people adhere to. Needless to say, I taught myself how to drive without his assistance years ago, going to a public library to go through an online driving course on the public access computers. My ultimate goal is to someday have enough money saved to buy a beater car with flat cash, which will give me much more freedom and independence from my father's control. And that, in turn, will allow me to take better care of my sisters.

Which is why I really ought to be spending today trolling for a job, not tearing across town on some drunken goose chase with my dad.

"Will we be back in time for lunch? Because there isn't any food in the house and the girls are hungry," I keep going, trying to keep my voice even. I've learned to control my tone and demeanor, adjusting my attitude to suit whatever mood my dad is in at the moment. It's so easy to accidentally set him off that I have become a master mind reader.

I can tell from the moment my dad walks through the door what state of mind he's in. And even when I am bristling with rage or on the verge of tears, I can make my voice sound peppy, sweet, and totally innocent. It's a good skill to have, and one that has truly allowed me to survive despite my dad's tendency toward violence. Especially now that I'm older. When I was a kid, he wasn't as intimidated by me. He knew his word was the final word and I would have no way of defying him. But nowadays, he's weirdly self-conscious and insecure, because deep down he knows that I am more intelligent and competent than he is. I'm not a little girl anymore, and I don't really need him at all. So if he detects even the slightest hint of condescension or defiance in my voice, he loses his mind.

So, I have adapted to make myself sound as naive and gentle as possible.

"Oh, no. This is an all-day affair, Peanut!" Dad exclaims, and I wince at the use of his old nickname for me. It's not that I think I'm too old or too cool for a cutesy nickname or anything. It's just that it reminds me of a time when things were better, back when he said that nickname with real affection.

"Could we possibly swing by later and bring them some food then, maybe? It's just that I feel guilty having a fun birthday with my dad while Daisy and Sunny are at home—"

I am interrupted by my dad smacking his hand hard on the steering wheel, making me jump. He gives me a cold glare, his jaw clenching. "Forget about the brats for five fucking minutes, will you?" he demands, rifling his hand back through his greasy dark hair. I can't remember the last time I noticed him use the shower at the house.

"Sorry, Daddy," I say quietly, folding my hands in my lap and looking away out the window. He chuckles grimly.

"Damn it, Peanut. You always know just how to push your poor old dad's buttons, don't ya? Always have. Sorry, kiddo," he says, not sounding even remotely sorry. I know his apologies are just empty words by now, mocking and meaningless. He can apologize a million times without changing a single thing about himself.

We ride in silence for a while longer, the van rumbling down the road. I dare not ask again where the hell we are headed, and it seems to me like we're going in the opposite direction of all my dad's favorite bars. We aren't even going in the direction of Atlantic City. We seem to be going northeast, from the signs we're passing.

We stop briefly at a liquor store, my dad telling me, "Sit tight. I'm just gonna go in and grab a six pack. Nothin' too crazy, but you ought to let loose on your birthday!"

I don't drink. At least, I never have before, except for when my dad has forced me to join him for a beer on the back porch. I think he just gets lonely sometimes, and he wants someone else to fall down this terrible rabbit hole with him so he doesn't feel so alone and pathetic. He's suffering, and he wants everyone else to suffer with him. Especially me. He's always making comments about how much we're alike, how I'm just the girl version of him. I don't see it, except for in my looks, but I would not dare tell him he's wrong.

And I am terrified of turning out just like him. So alcohol has always been off-limits for me. Besides, I still have three more years before I can legally drink — not that laws have ever stopped my dad from doing whatever the hell he wants.

A few minutes later, he emerges with a six-pack of Budweiser's and hops into the driver's seat, twisting a bottle open and handing it over to me. I reluctantly take it from him, hoping he won't notice if I just refuse to drink any of it. But to my dismay, he gives me a nod of encouragement and says, "Go on! Take a swig! It's your birthday, damn it."

"Yeah, but I'm only turning eighteen, Daddy. Not twenty-one," I remark, forcing myself to smile. He rolls his eyes and starts the car, waving his hand to urge me to do it anyway.

"Those laws don't mean nothin' for people like you and me," he comments, cracking open a bottle for himself, even though he's driving. Frank Barnes has no qualms about driving under the influence, nor driving with an open container. It's a miracle he's never been pulled over and arrested for either of those things. Actually, it's more like a curse. I keep hoping one of these days he'll get arrested and that will knock some sense into him.

But I know that will never happen. He's too far gone. He would rather die drunk in a holding cell than live sober. Because if his mind is clear, he's forced to be alone with his thoughts, and I think that's a fate worse than death for my father.

Finally, I oblige him by having a sip, bending down so that I can hide it a little better from any passing cars. Dad lets out a whoop of satisfaction, grinning proudly.

"That's my girl! We're gonna have a good time today, kiddo," he says, turning on the radio. An old Stevie Ray Vaughan song comes on and Dad starts singing along in his usual loud, off-key tenor. I remember laughing at his singing as a kid, giggling hysterically as he tried unsuccessfully to sing along with my mother, who had the voice of an angel. Sure, he might have sounded awful back then, but at least there was spirit in his voice. He was happy then, and my mom was just happy to have someone sing with her, even if he couldn't stay on beat or hit the right note.

Nowadays, his singing just breaks my heart. His throat has been ravaged by years of alcohol abuse, and he pauses between verses to take long, deep swigs of his beer. I slump down in the seat and take the occasional sip of my own bottle, staring morosely out the window as we rattle down the highway. I wonder if he even has a game plan in mind, or if we're just joyriding for the hell of it. Either way, I can't get my mind off of Sunny and Daisy. I just know their little stomachs are growling, and every minute they're home alone causes me extreme anxiety. I should be there for them. I should be home.

We ride for about two hours, my dad getting progressively more intoxicated and louder as the time wears on. We cross over the state line into New York, and by now I am abandoning any hopes of being home for lunch time. Or even dinner. I have a feeling we're going to be gone for quite some time, and I curse myself inwardly for not going out and buying food with the last of my meager savings yesterday, while I still had the chance.

Finally, we find ourselves chugging along a road that hugs the coastline, the sandy beaches in plain sight through my window. I notice that we're not too far from the Big Apple, approaching an area I believe is called Brighton Beach. We pull to a stop in a parking lot adjacent to a big, fancy harbor. The docks are filled with tourists and pot-bellied men with their much younger and blonder arm candy. Pure white sails and high masts stretch into the bright blue sky, dark waves rocking the boats from below.

"What are we doing here?" I ask, frowning in confusion.

"Going on a little boat ride, Peanut!" my dad declares, sliding out of the driver's seat and coming around to yank me out of the passenger's side. Dressed in my simple black leggings and oversized red-and-black plaid flannel, I feel extremely out of place here. And my dad, in his stained white T-shirt and musty old jeans, looks more like a homeless man than a yachtsman. For a minute, I am paralyzed with the fear that my dad has truly lost it — maybe he's brought us here with some bizarre fantasy of stealing a sailboat. I really could not put it past him to do that.

But when he takes me by the hand and pulls me along to the wooden docks, he seems to know exactly where he's going. Like he's actually planned something, for once in his life. For a split second, I wonder if maybe he really has somehow booked us a bizarre birthday boat tour or something. However, when we end up boarding a boat filled with loud music, booze, and half-naked women accompanying various sleazily-dressed men to makeshift craps and blackjack tables on the deck... I realize why we're really here. This is just another venue for my dad to gamble. Of course, I can't quite figure out why the hell he needs to have me with him to do this, but there's no way I can ask him without inciting his rage.

We're both severely underdressed, but while a few of the beautiful and Botoxed women give us curious glances, everyone else pretty much accepts us. I wonder who the hell would allow my dad on such a fancy, elaborate boat. Who does he know here? How did he manage to land us a place on this yacht?

"Come on, Peanut. You're my good luck charm today," Dad says, grabbing my arm and pulling me over to a cards table, plopping me down in a deck chair beside him. A busty brunette deals out the cards and I use this opportunity to survey our surroundings. There's a table of gourmet hors d'oeuvres and expensive champagne, as well as a couple stiff-backed waiters making the rounds with trays of croquettes. A vaguely European club beat is pounding from below deck, lending a further air of sleaze to the whole scene. Older men are flanked on both sides by beautiful women, left and right.

My heart sinks a little when I notice that we're leaving the docks, heading out onto the deep blue bay. This looks to be some kind of pleasure cruise for gamblers — something right up my father's alley, even if the decor and dress code are leagues higher than his usual fare.

And still... I don't understand why I need to be here with him.

We spend the entire day out on the water, which I admit is almost nice in a cautious kind of way. I pile a plate with delicate little quiches and fritters, finally filling my stomach after so long without a solid meal. Of course, I do so with a heavy sense of guilt, knowing the twins are at home going hungry. I make a silent vow to myself to never let the household be empty of food ever again, even if it means having to steal.

In the evening, just as the sun is beginning to set, we pull back into the docks. Most of the people leave immediately, but my dad slithers an arm around my shoulders and says, "Time for us to go down below deck. There's something I have to do."

His tone is light, but I can detect something sinister lurking just below the surface. I'm instantly on guard, knowing that whatever my father has planned cannot be anything good. But he's almost giddy as we walk down the steps into a stately room with classical music playing from a fancy stereo system. The furnishings are lush and velvety, a chandelier hanging from the center of the ceiling. This place looks more like the inside of a swanky hotel room than the below deck of a boat, even one as elaborate as this.

A group of brutish-looking, burly men stand up from a round mahogany table when we enter the room, all of them eyeing me with a kind of ravenous awe. I swallow hard, fear gathering in my core. My heart races as my dad says, "I did what I was told. I got her here. Your guy is gonna hold up his end of the bargain, right? I need to be sure before I let my baby girl go."

"What?" I burst out, pushing away from him. I feel sick to my stomach. What the hell does he mean, *let me go?*

Underneath his flippant attitude and the veil of drunkenness, there is a twinge of pain in my father's eyes, and I know this is for real. This is not a joke. He is giving me away. But in what way?

One man steps forward from the group and looks me up and down with a critical expression. "I would have expected you to present her in a more, ah, appealing manner," husks the man in a cruel voice. There's a heavy Russian accent coloring his words.

"You sayin' my girl ain't pretty enough?" my dad says, bristling defensively.

"No, no, she is sufficient. But even a diamond may not shine if it is covered with dirt," the man quips, clearly referring to the dowdy, shapeless flannel shirt that hangs down nearly to my knees.

"Oh, you mean the clothes? Well, this is really the best we got," Dad remarks, shrugging. Then he reaches over and nudges me. "Take off that shirt, Peanut. Show 'em what's underneath."

I stare at him, slack-jawed, for a long moment. I cannot believe what he's asking of me. This has to be some kind of nightmare that I will wake up from any minute now. I know my father is a drunken, useless son of a bitch, but I never expected him to do something like this.

"Now, Rosalie!" he orders, taking an aggressive step toward me. I shrink away and immediately start to obey, unbuttoning my flannel shirt with shaking hands and letting it fall to the ground so that I'm standing before this group of strangers in my tight black leggings and threadbare sports bra. The leader of the group purses his lips and nods in apparent approval.

"She will certainly do," he appraises, rubbing his chin thoughtfully. "Nice doing business with you, Mister Barnes. Now, get the hell out."

"My debts are paid off?" my father asks.

The man rolls his eyes, regarding him with pure disgust. "Yes. In full. Leave."

"You got it," Dad replies, with a flourish and a bow. He gives me a nod as he turns to leave, his final words to me falling limply from his mouth: "Be good, Peanut. Daddy's sorry."

"No!" I shout, running after him as he disappears up the stairs to the top deck. But two of the men rush forward and grab my arms, holding me in place while I scream in horror.

"Be quiet. The deal is done," commands the leader.

"Please, there has to be something else I can do — I need to go home — there are two little girls who need me," I plead, tears burning in my eyes. "How long do I have to stay here? They're hungry and alone! You have to let me go, please!"

"Want me to shut her up, boss?" growls the man on my right.

"We can soften her up for the client, break her in a little," offers the man on my left.

The leader shakes his head. "No, no. She must be kept in pristine condition for the Bull. He will want her untouched, for certain. You know how it is. Some men like their jewels polished and set, but others prefer a diamond in the rough."

"Who is the Bull?" I ask, tears coursing down my cheeks.

The leader looks back at me as he walks away to make a call on his cell phone, giving me an almost bemused expression. "Ah, the bitch is eager. But you will find out soon enough."

KONSTANTIN

*W*e'd arrived at the yacht in a limousine while Anton showed me pictures of what was to be my very own condo suite. He wasn't kidding about its accommodations.

"Again," he'd said, "all of this is only temporary. If you wish, Sergei's manor will soon be ready for your personal use. There are just a few things we need to take care of there before letting you have free reign of the place, you understand."

Clean the blood out of the carpets and make sure none of Sergei's dirty laundry is too easy for me to find. I'd understood his meaning perfectly, and I knew that this was standard procedure for power changes. My job as an effective leader would involve finding out what I could from the pieces that were left over from the cleanup, though.

Now that I'm onboard the yacht, I'm in a position

to start doing just that. The view from the top deck is just as stunning as the view of the yacht was from down below. It was almost a comfort to know that the sleazy, decadence of wealthy Russian tastes hardly changed in the United States. The golden letters spelling out the ship's name, *The Tsar's Palace*, told me that much.

I'm wearing the same clothes I did when I stepped off the plane, unlike Anton, who stepped into a bathroom to change in the airport, and I suspect I'm still the best-dressed person on the yacht. My tailored black suit might be tight-fitting, and I've long since abandoned my tie to unbutton the top of the red shirt under it and free my neck, but I'm not wearing the leisure suit so many of the other patrons seem to be sporting, and that's a fact I pride myself on.

Music fills the air as I walk with Anton across the deck, the clinking of glasses and cheering of drunken voices all around me immersing me in the purest atmosphere of a Russian celebration I could hope for.

"I take it this is routine for Russian-Americans?" I say quietly to Anton as we walk, and he gives a boisterous laugh. I don't know where the glass of vodka in his hand came from, but it's already half-empty.

"You'll find the accommodations here a little more upbeat than what you're used to back home, my friend," he says with a warm smile. "It's something to get used to. It'll be a little uncomfortable at first, I promise you that, but that thick accent will drop the more you enjoy everything the USA has to offer."

I'm not sure how much I like the sound of that, but I nod, glancing around the crowds that revel under the dark sky, the stars blotted out by the city's looming skyline lights. I see a variety of faces among the Russians, a few of them important men I recognize from back home. I've met precious few of them, while others have even been clients of mine, and we must avoid eye contact. Such are the politics of the Bratva. The older men are accompanied by lovely young women, almost uniformly. All of them are dressed exquisitely, their hair and makeup painstakingly arranged, and I wonder how many of them are here of their own free will.

"Ladies and gentlemen," Anton says as we near the center of the deck, "everyone, your attention, please! Our guest of honor has arrived — show some respect!"

Heads start to turn to us, and I start doling out nods of acknowledgement. I'm easily the tallest man in the room, and several of the people in the crowd had already taken notice, so surveying the crowd around me is a simple thing. The DJ lowers the music, and Anton stands in front of me, beaming broadly as a couple of other burly men make their way out of the crowd to stand at his side while he announces me.

I'm not oblivious to the fact that Anton is making a show of riding my coattails tonight. He's always been a diplomatic type, serving as advisors to other higher-ups around the world throughout his career. I suspect there's something deep inside him seething about my promotion, but for the time being, his support is important.

"I don't want you all to forget why we're here tonight," he says, lowering his voice to a speaking volume as the crowd quiets down. "This is an exciting time for us, a time for inspiring change and greater fortunes than ever before, both for those of you born and bred here in America," he says with a nod to several of the guests who raise their glasses respectfully back, "and for those of us fresh off the boat," he grins back to me. There will be little or no mention of the Bratva specifically, of course. This is hardly mixed company, but it's in poor taste to speak 'publically' about what it is we do.

"And tonight, we raise a glass to our newly arrived associate who will help us realize this dream of a brighter tomorrow. My dear friends and colleagues, the esteemed Mr. Konstantin Alkaev!" There's a scattered applause as Anton introduces me with a comically sweeping gesture, and I force a smile, nodding to those around me and raising a modest hand. This kind of pageantry is hardly the kind of business I feel comfortable conducting. I can already tell that the mantle of leadership will feel uncomfortable on my shoulders. I have been a leader of men in the past. Maybe I'll flourish doing it again. But I'm a man of action, first and foremost, and not even this position could keep me in an armchair if I wanted to let it.

"Thank you all," I say, my deep voice showing my heavy Russian accent as I pronounce the English words slowly, with Anton gesturing for me to say something. "I am not one for speeches, but I look forward to getting to know you all as we move forward." I know that what's about to follow is a tedious series of introductions to rancid old men I'd rather not deal with at all. "*Zazdarovje!*"

"*Zazdarovje!*" the Russian-speaking crowd raises a glass along with me, and there's a scattered applause as the music resumes.

What follows is a surprisingly lighthearted affair. I was expecting to be ushered to the side immediately, but the people seem amenable to enjoying the party as I make my way to the bar and start celebrating with the crowd.

Of introductions, though, there is no shortage. With Anton and his two bodyguards — my two bodyguards as well, I realize — I'm greeted by everyone who is anyone in Brighton Beach. The top arms smuggler in the region shakes my hand and shares a drink with me as we reminisce over an old job we did together back in St. Petersburg when I was first getting started. A small-time politician who happens to be the son of one of the more influential Bratva leaders in New England greets me like a son, giving me a tight embrace and giving me a rundown on the political climate around Brighton. One of my former clients, a man who paid me to eliminate one of the most notorious narcotics kingpins in Russia, even approaches me — introducing himself as if for the first time, of course — and tells me what a pleasure it will be to have me so close to home.

One by one, as the vodka flows and the dancing becomes less restrained, men of the Bratva come to pay their respects to me. It's a truly strange feeling. I've lived in the shadows my entire life, from the cold streets of Moscow to the wretched walls of a prison, and now, it's my skill at hunting human lives that has gained the fear of all those around me.

In time, once the more important people have made their rounds introducing themselves and meeting one another, Anton finds me again, having wandered off to speak to a few others.

"I hope everything is to your liking, *pakhan*," he says in a low tone, a broad smile on his face as he addresses me by my new title. I give him a light chuckle, clapping him on the back as I step away from the bar. "Everything easy on the eyes?"

"I'm not used to having so much carried out in

my honor," I say truthfully, "but it would be immodest to ask for a better welcome to America."

"I mean the *girls*, Konstantin," he says, his eyes narrowing and his smile broadening as he gives a nod to the crowd.

There are a few women by the dance floor, talking to each other, in dresses whose necks plunge down deep at the collar, and I watch Anton ravish them with his eyes. In truth, I've hardly had time to speak to the women here, not that I hadn't intended to do just that when I got half a breath, but the way Anton carries himself makes me less than eager to conduct myself in any way that could associate me with him.

"They're lovely," I say simply, catching the eye of one of them across the room, and she flashes me a shy smile before saying something to her friend with a blush. I have an intimidating presence, but Anton's words make me wonder how many of the women here are being paid for, and how many were simply bought.

"If you think they're lovely," he says, and I can already anticipate what his next words are going to be, "then I have a sight for you. Come, I have something special to show you."

Before I can say anything further, he nods towards the doors of the yacht that lead to the elevators, and I follow him in, pushing past a few other half-drunken guests vying for my attention. He walks past the elevators to a door that has a guard posted at it, who nods at both of us before opening the door and standing aside. I notice that Anton's two guards are absent as we approach.

"What is the meaning of all this, Anton?" I ask as we step inside, but he only smiles back at me as the room comes into view.

The room we're in now is like the penthouse of an apartment, built into the yacht. It's dimly lit, with ample open space and hardwood floors stretching to what seems to be the back of the ship, judging by the window on the far side of the room with an unimpeded view of the bay outside. Lovely artwork hangs from the walls, and planters overflowing with vibrant plants sit below them. There's even a small, inactive hot tub in the middle of the room. It's clearly the closest thing to a VIP suite this club of a yacht has.

The first two people in the room I notice are burly men, not unlike Anton's guards who followed us around all day. One stands on the inside of the door, regarding us silently as we enter. The other stands behind one of the couches, his thickly muscled arms crossed.

On the couch in front of him is the most beautiful woman I've ever laid eyes on.

Her pale skin seems to stand out like a centerpiece in the darkness around her, somehow at once infused with it yet distinct from it, and the ocean-blue eyes that look up at me are bursting with the kind of knowing fear that wrenches at my heart — a despondent look tempered by hardship yet ever more surprised at the depths of depravity its owner has been exposed to. She's dressed — or rather half-undressed — simply, her exposed bra and leggings making her look fresh off the street. Everything about her tells me she's never imagined being where she is tonight in her wildest dreams, or her worst nightmares.

I wonder if the empathy I feel swelling within me shows through my stony killer's gaze. It only lasts half an instant before Anton shuts the door behind us.

"I know this isn't really your kind of thing," he says, a wicked smile on his face, "but the men and I thought that you deserved a proper welcome to America — something the plastic opulence outside can't provide."

I watch Anton stalk around the room toward the couch. There are two other couches on either side, and he rests his hands on the one to the right as the other muscle stands aside to give me an unimpeded view of the young woman.

"So I thought I'd take the liberty of arranging this little party favor for you," he says pleasantly, stepping over towards her to take her by the chin. She glares daggers at him as he turns her around, showing off her straight, dark hair. Her expression seems to be muted by default, and I can't blame her. So much of her beauty resides in the fury she can muster in that look she aims at Anton, even though she's powerless to act on it.

"You're kind," I say, guarding my tone carefully, showing as little emotion as I can, "but I must refuse your generous offer. You've done more than enough to show your respects today, Anton."

"Ah, but you don't understand," he says, raising his eyebrows and turning her face to look at me as he does. "This American gem was not easy to arrange, my friend. As you can see, she's truly one of a kind, fresh and unbroken, an untouched virgin. And when I say that she's *your* party favor for tonight," he says, withdrawing his hand from her at last and stepping back, "I *mean* that she is yours. This young woman is your tribute for your new role — she belongs to you, now."

"Then I will do with her as I wish," I say firmly, stepping forward towards the couches. The young woman's eyes are on me, the careful gaze of a wounded deer being approached by its predator. "Would you interfere with your *pakhan*'s wishes?"

"Well, sir," Anton says, folding his hands behind his back, "I can see that you *really* don't understand." He lets his hands part, and that's when I see the glint of the pistol in his hand as he points it at me from his hip, as casually as if he'd been taking out a cigarette lighter. Our gazes meet coldly, and to see the veneer of politeness drop from his eyes would have been a relief under any other circumstances. "We're all delighted to have you in America, make no mistake. But a few people — myself included — have some...concerns, regarding your reputation."

I don't dignify Anton with a response, my hard gaze even on him.

"As I have said, things are changing rapidly in Brighton Beach," he says, "and certain parties want to be sure that you are indeed the right man to lead us there. Assurances have to be made. Proven," he adds, his thumb brushing over the chamber of the gun as he brushes the barrel through the woman's hair. Her eyes widen as she realizes what Anton is holding, and they flit up to me, wanting to look to me for help yet remembering all too soon that I'm as much her predator as Anton is.

"So, my friend," Anton says, his voice chillingly casual as he takes a seat on the couch to the right, gun raised, "come and show this lovely young lady what a real Russian man can do." My gaze shifts from Anton to the woman whose name I don't even know, her form laid out on the couch like a reluctant offering. She's beautiful beyond words, and I cannot deny my desire for her, but she is not here willingly. She is not giving herself to me, she is being given. She is a slave to the mob.

And I have to fuck her, or we'll both die tonight.

"Do it now, or you'll be fucking a corpse," orders one of the mafia men quietly, the barrel of his gun pointed directly at the side of my head. The man in front of me clenches his jaw in anger, clearly struggling with this moral dilemma. It's little comfort to know that at least he doesn't *want* to give into this absurd, horrifying deal. Some small, insecure voice in the back of my head whispers that maybe he just doesn't want to fuck *me*, in particular. Maybe he doesn't find me attractive.

It's ridiculous that even in a life or death situation, my mind has room for insecurities.

Even with a gun aimed at my brain, it continues to generate self-conscious thoughts.

I snap myself out of that and remind myself that this guy probably isn't even thinking about whether

I'm sexually desirable or not. He's got more than enough to worry about, with the number of weapons poised to destroy us both. I decide to make things a little easier on him.

"It's okay," I whisper faintly, and the man turns to look at me with such luminescent sorrow shining in his stormy gray eyes. They remind me of gathering rain clouds, of deep and churning waters in old-timey paintings of shipwrecks. His eyes are the color of trouble, of bad omens and dark shadows. But I need him to trust me, at least until we get out of this mess.

I can tell he wants me to trust him, too, but this current predicament is testing us both.

If we don't do this, it's certain death. But if we do… what will become of us then? Or me at least?

After all, I'm a virgin; I don't even know what I'm supposed to do with my body under normal circumstances, much less at gunpoint.

"I am sorry for this," he murmurs in response, his voice low and thrumming. It sends a tremble through my core, every nerve in my body on alert. It's like he's spoken some kind of magical incantation, muting and blurring the world surrounding us in an instant, leaving just the two of us standing before each other in a shared, soft vibration.

He steps forward, raising one hesitant hand to brush the heavy, dark hair back from my face, those gray eyes searching me with desperation, a hint of pleading.

And then he kisses me. I sigh into his mouth, my body stiffening at first, and then melting into his waiting arms. Somewhere, distantly, I am still cognizant of the guns pointed at us and the men watching us without even the slightest thread of decency or guile. But in this moment, those are all mere background observations to be shelved and explored at a later time. All I can do right now is lean into this kiss, my first real kiss, and try to remember to breathe.

Every cell in my body has come alive.

I feel myself rising, warmth tingling into my limbs and setting my heart rate a tick faster. The man — the Bull — wraps me in his arms and strokes my hair, his lips surprisingly soft and gentle against mine compared to his hard body. His hands slip down to grasp my hips, maneuvering me even closer so that we're pressed fully against each other. I can feel his hardening length pushing into my thigh and a little thrill of mingled interest and fear passes through me.

"I can make this quick for you," he says softly, his breath tickling the exposed skin of my neck. "And as painless as I can manage."

Somehow, all of my words have gotten lost somewhere between my brain and my lips, and so I simply nod my assent instead. In one swift, fluid movement, he cradles me back into his forearms and gently lays me down on the floor, crouching over me in a stance that would have been predatory if not for the twinge of apology in his eyes.

He bends down to kiss me again, his lips soft at first, then more insistent. My own lips part to allow his tongue access, our mouths moving together in probing curiosity. There is a static current running between us as his hands rove up and down my body, gently caressing my bare stomach and partially exposed breasts. I feel a certain respect and reverence in his every motion, as though I'm the one in control despite lying here submissive to him. Like he's almost afraid of breaking me. He touches me like I'm a pristine forest and his fingertips ignite fires.

But the men watching us are totally numb to our tender exploration of each other's bodies. The leader groans impatiently and hisses, "Move it along. We don't have all night."

The Bull's hand tightens into a fist at the side of my hair, twisting a lock of my hair over his thick knuckles. I can tell from this one small movement that he is a reservoir of incredible fury and strength, which he must actively work to keep levied back. Behind the veil of calm lurks an awe-inspiring power, betrayed only in part by the dark clouds in his eyes.

He breaks away from our kiss momentarily,

those eyes grazing over my face in hungry paths. He then slides a hand underneath my back to deftly unclasp my bra, slipping it back over my head. I feel my entire body flush with humiliation as the three other men stand by watching. Their cruel, greedy lust is palpable. I feel like a slab of bloody steak laid before three ravenous coyotes.

But to my relief and gratitude, the Bull strips off his own black jacket and perfectly-pressed white shirt to lean over me, blocking my bare chest from their lewd gaze. His own broad, sculpted chest rippling with muscles, inked with ominous tattoos that excite as much as they make me fear him.

I hold my breath in fear and wonder of what might happen next. I have seen movies, of course, and I know the general mechanics of making love. But this, being in the position myself, feels totally foreign. I am a pretty capable woman, and I always assumed I would know exactly what to do when the time came. But I'm realizing that I need the Bull's guidance. More than that… I crave it.

His hands gently grip my breasts, dragging in slow circles over my sensitive nipples. I let out an unbidden moan and a flash of animalistic desire flickers for a brief second in his gray eyes. I stare up at him in unabashed curiosity, watching him watch me.

"Hurry up," barks the leader of the mafia guys. I glance over to see that he's got the gun pointed at us again, and it's obvious that the Bull has taken notice of this, too, as he quickly pulls down my leggings and unzips his black trousers. His cock springs free and my eyes go wide at the unexpected size of it. I always thought they would be smaller. But this is monstrous. I can feel my flower clenching up in fear at the prospect of something so huge trying to ram its way in.

But mingled with that fear is a strange desire.

I want him to fuck me. For all the years I lived for nothing more than taking care of my sisters, did nothing for myself, I wanted to feel alive.

It goes beyond a simple, understandable sense of self-preservation. It's more than that. But I don't get much of an opportunity to think about it before the Bull tugs down my panties and pushes my thighs apart to let the head of his enormous shaft rub against my dampening slit. I involuntarily buck up into the point of contact, feeling a sudden, over-whelming need to be closer.

"I wish things could be different," he murmurs to me, barely audible. And with that, he reaches down to position himself at my opening, and pushes inside with one deep thrust.

An electric current of pain jolts through my body and I cry out, clutching in vain at the smooth floor on either side of me. Tears sting in my eyes and I hear the three onlookers chuckle in satisfaction.

They are enjoying this, watching my pain and humiliation.

But the Bull is shockingly responsive to my agony, leaning down to kiss my lips, my cheeks, my forehead, his hands smoothing back my hair and cupping my cheeks in a comforting fashion. He slowly pulls back out and then spears me again, the pain only marginally decreased this time. Hot tears spill down my cheeks and into the floorboards, wetting my hair. The Bull reaches down to softly massage the tight bundle of nerves at the top of my slit, sending a shock of intense pleasure through me. As he continues the small, consistent circle, he pumps into me slowly at first, then picks up the pace. Agony subsides slightly, being overridden by a mounting ecstasy as he works my clit and pushes against a deep, dark spot within my cunt. Finally, with a strangled cry, a wave of bliss overcomes me and I twitch violently, fumbling to grasp at his arms and shoulders.

And then he loses control, pumping into me as though my own climax has freed the rabid beast inside of him. He pounds into my pussy with abandon, groaning and murmuring in slurred Russian. Finally, while my cunt still shudders with orgasm, he releases a hot stream of seed into me, groaning wantonly. He bends down to kiss me, our bodies heaving together under the unwavering gaze of our three hideous bystanders.

"Well done," appraises the leader, clapping his hands slowly. "Now get up and get yourselves cleaned up. It's time to go."

"We will return in a moment," adds one of his henchmen as all three of them turn and walk out of the cabin, leaving me alone and naked with the Bull.

After a moment, he helps me to my feet and hands me my clothing, then quickly puts his own clothes back on. "I wish it did not have to be this way," he says earnestly, sadness coloring his tone.

I still cannot muster a single word, like my voice has suddenly disappeared.

Slipping his jacket over his thick, muscular arms, he continues: "I am not one of them, I promise you. Perhaps at one time I thought I was allied with them, but those days are now past. I have tried to make amends for what I've done. You must understand, I am not one of them. Not anymore. I have made it my mission to rescue the girls these pigs wish to imprison and treat like mere property. I never would have done this if I thought there was any other way."

I can only nod, unable to make eye contact with him. I feel so broken, so exposed, now that the adrenaline rush is subsiding. The Bull steps closer and I fall back. He looks genuinely hurt.

In a softer voice, he says, "I will do whatever is in my power to protect you. I refuse to let them hurt you any further. I don't know how you got here or why, but I swear to you, I will save you from this however I can." He holds out his hand for me to shake, and I hesitantly take it.

"My name is Konstantin."

Finally, I lift my gaze to meet his eyes. "I'm Rosie."

That's a lovely name, I want to tell her, but it feels like such a trite thing to tell her here and now. The word lingers on my tongue when the door opens again, and once her clothes are back on, I realize she's still lacking a top. "Do you have a shirt?"

"They took it," she says after a moment of processing my question. I nod, and without another word, I slip my fitted jacket off my shoulders. She winces for a moment, afraid, but she stands still as I drape it over her shoulders, and she instinctively pulls it around her to cover herself.

"It may be a little large on you," I say, and it's a gross understatement. She looks like a bat blinking up at me, the bottom of the jacket dangling halfway down her thighs, and the sleeves could totally cover her hands if they weren't bunched back. "But it will have to do for now."

She hesitates, then gives a quick nod, leaving silence between us again for a tense moment. Then Anton strides in, this time accompanied by one of the older men I met during the party.

"Ah," he says, beaming as if nothing of this sort had just happened, and I'm canny enough to play along for the time being, turning and regarding him casually. "I'm glad to see the two of you getting along. There are a few more friends of ours I wanted to introduce you to now that we've gotten a few formalities out of the way. So please, why don't you come back on the deck with us? The yacht is heading back to port, but we have a few minutes still."

I nod calmly, and before Anton can utter another word, I turn to Rosie and nod cordially for her to follow me. She looks bewildered, but I give her a meaningful look. I then turn my eyes back to Anton, who casts me a glare, but his mind for decorum doesn't allow him to argue with me just now.

"And of course," he says, broadening his fake smile, "your new friend is more than welcome to accompany you, even if she is a little 'comfortably' dressed," he adds, as if it's her fault she doesn't have a gaudy track suit to blend in with the rest of the 'high society' present.

Rosie gives me a reluctant look, but I do my best to appear as comforting to her as I can as I motion for her to follow me out the door and into the crowd of people, many of whom would be just as apt to do what I was just forced to do at gunpoint.

This is all a power play on the Bratva factions scrambling to keep things together in Sergei's wake, I understand immediately. I feel a heavy weight in my heart as I realize the full gravity of the situation. Anton has dispelled any notion of my heroics by forcing me to do what I did, perhaps even trying to worm his way into my head. And he's just the tip of the iceberg, as far as I know. As I guide Rosie through the crowd, I cast glances around me, meeting roving eyes that regard me briefly as we emerge from the lounge. I wonder how many of those eyes know what's just taken place and plan to use it against me.

But I am not a man to be blackmailed. If they think they can use this kind of vulgar stunt against me, they have something else coming — something they won't be prepared to handle.

Even I cannot stave off the guilt of what I've done, though. As Anton guides us to whoever the hell he means to introduce me to next, I reach out to take Rosie's hand, and she lets it happen, numbly, her fingers cold as ice and her arm listless.

She was enslaved. She was defenseless. She was scared. And I violated her.

I glance behind me and see a blank look on her face. She follows me as if through a dream as we navigate the crowd, and I know there's nowhere else in the world she'd find less pleasant than here at my side, but somehow, her legs carry her on, maybe driven by the thought that I'm better than being at the mercy of whatever strangers who handled her on her way up here. I might be her captor now, but if it means keeping her safe, I won't let her out of my sight.

My thoughts are entirely on how she must be feeling right now, and I know I can never begin to understand the whirlwind of emotion — or lack thereof — and the effect it's having on her at this very moment. I'm only half-present as Anton starts to introduce me to yet another group of old men, and the small talk resumes as if nothing so vile had ever taken place just a few minutes ago. The best I can do is to try and protect her...but how can I do that when she's my victim?

Hours later, the yacht party is finally behind us, and I'm heading out onto the dock parking lot with Rosie, accompanied by the guard who'd been standing outside the lounge when I was brought inside.

"As he may have mentioned," says the man as the Brighton breeze cools us off, our voices echoing in the spacious parking lot, "Anton has a car arranged for you. I hope it's to your liking, and I can assure you, it's top of the line by local standards."

I raise my eyebrows as we approach a sleek black luxury sedan, its windows tinted and its shine so pristine that the moonlight seems brighter for it. "It will do," I say with a nod as the man hands me the keys. I unlock it and lead Rosie to the passenger's side, where I help her in and close the door. She seems to just be staring ahead as I round the car and approach the guard again.

"I'm texting you the address of your apartment," he says, taking out his phone. "You should find everything to your liking there. But please, let me know if there's anything else we can provide."

There's a certain hesitation to his voice that I don't fail to notice. He's trying to keep his eyes from drifting to the young woman in the car, but it isn't a simple lust in his eyes. He almost looks conflicted, and I wonder how many of the people on the lower rungs of the hierarchy in Brighton would prefer to see such unsavory business be done away with.

"Thank you," I tell him with a curt nod. "I'll keep you in mind." My wording is deliberate. "But I understand that there is somewhere more suitable being prepared for me, yes?"

"Mr. Slokavich's old manor, yes sir," he says with a nod. "When it is ready, I hope you'll find it just as impressive as he did. Though his tastes were rather…"

I stop him, giving a simple understanding look, and he smiles back at me knowingly. "I would like to drive by it and see my future quarters. Text me its address as well."

"Of course, sir," he says, and with that, I dismiss him and step into the car.

We pull out into the night as I begin heading for the manor, and I glance over to Rosie before we head out into the open road. It's late, nearing midnight, but the streets of Brighton Beach are still rather busy.

"This city has a thriving night life," I comment after ten minutes of tense silence. I don't blame her for saying nothing, her gaze fixed on the window.

"Are you a native?" I ask, trying to check my thick accent, but I know it will be hard to keep from slipping out around her. I notice the faintest shake of her head that I've ever seen, but she says nothing. I frown a little, not because of her reluctance, but because that means she has no friends in the city who could help her.

I wonder how much she knows. Whether she has any idea who I am, where we're going, or what's to become of her. I wonder how much Anton put into her head in the short time she's been in captivity. I still don't know how long ago she was taken, but the numbness she still feels tells me she must be painfully fresh to this life.

But I will not give her what her deepest nightmares are expecting. That is why I have no intention of going to my suite tonight.

To make Rosie's silence a little more peaceful, I turn the radio on and let soft music play for the rest of the way to the manor, and I do my best not to look over at her. After what seems like an eternity, I finally see what must be the manor coming up ahead.

It's a lavish estate, and I can tell it's one Sergei Slokavich was ill-suited to, to say the least. The gardens around the outside are starting to become dilapidated and wilted, and I wonder whether he even bothered to hire a gardener or two or if he planned to let the whole outdoors turn to waste under his rule.

I can tell we aren't expected, as there are hardly any guards out and about. In Russia, such compounds as this have men patrolling the perimeter, the balconies, and even the rooftops, but here, I see only a couple of men at the doors, and their surprise at my headlights as I pull up the driveway tells me all I need to know.

"Stay here," I tell Rosie quietly before stepping out of the car and hailing the men as they approach.

"You've taken a wrong turn," one of the men shouts in heavily accented English as he steps forward.

"Do you know who I am?" I reply in Russian,

startling them. The man who spoke squints at me, and his eyes widen in recognition.

"Mr. Alkaev?" They exchange glances and stand up a little straighter. "We weren't told to expect you yet."

"I know," I say, "there's been a change of plans. You are dismissed for the night. Say nothing of this to your superiors until the morning, I do not wish to be disturbed tonight. And remember who your *new* superior is. Understood?"

They hesitate a moment, then give curt nods, one of them handing me his key before trudging off towards their cars as I watch them depart. I then make my way to the car and open the door for Rosie, who seems understandably confused by everything she just watched in silence.

"I thought you'd prefer less large men with guns tonight," I say, trying to reassuring her lightly. "I think you've had your fill for a lifetime."

We make our way into the manor, and I stride in as though I've owned the place since its construction. Anton wasn't lying about one thing — the place is certainly still in disarray. I see boxes lining some of the walls at the entryway, and there are places where marks on the walls and floors are being repaired. But I know a large part of the renovation is a cover for cleaning out any secrets Sergei might have had.

I will busy myself with that investigation later.

For now, I have a more pressing matter at hand, and she's looking around the manor in awe. It's clear she's never been in a place so lavish as this.

"There are a few things I'd like to see changed, too," I admit as if in response to her gaze, and she blinks at me as if seeing me for the first time. I look at her sympathetically, then nod to the staircase at the far end of the entry hall. "Come, let's find your bed for the night."

I lead her up the stairs, hoping that I have the right idea of where the master bedroom is. After what feels like half a week of climbing, we reach the ornate wooden doors that tell me my suspicions were correct. Pushing them open, I can't help but grimace at what I see.

To most people, I'm sure this room looks like the lap of luxury. To me, it's an extravagant eyesore. The massive bed sports red sheets and silken pillows, and there are spare sheets sticking out from under the bed. There is a large, golden rug beneath it that I want to hurl out the window, and the embroidered curtains cover a few large windows. On the far left, there are two large glass doors that lead to a spacious balcony. There are the usual amenities one would expect from a bedroom, but each one looks like it's worth about what I would spend on an entire room. Stifling my embarrassment, I step into the room and gesture to the bed.

"You may stay here tonight," I say. "Forgive the

disarray, but you should find everything you need in this house, and of course, you're free to explore as much of it as you want." *I'll have to do some exploring myself, in the morning,* I think, but I don't want to burden her with the details of how precarious my position is right now.

She makes her way past me to the bed, eyeing it for a moment before taking an experimental seat on it. She then nods as if in approval, slipping my jacket off and setting it aside as she slips her shoes off and pulls her legs up under her.

"Thanks," she says, and she hasn't spoken in so long that her voice sounds almost unfamiliar, tinted with caution. Her hooded eyes look up to me again, and she starts to speak, but stops herself. After a moment, I give a nod in reply.

"Rosie," I say, and the name is a little strange on my tongue, but I like the way it comes out. "Know that I meant what I said. I cannot take back what has happened to you. Nor what those men did to you and told you to expect. But I will not do so much as sleep in the same bed as you unless you wish it." She keeps her gaze on me, and I wonder whether she believes me. "I have to make some calls," I say, starting to move towards the exit. "You are welcome to do as you please. When I walk out those doors, my back will be to you. Should you choose to leave this place, I won't pursue you, and I will make up some story for the men you saw on the yacht."

I pause, looking her in those wide, surprised eyes. "So if this is the last time we see each other...farewell."

I turn to head out the wooden door to the bedroom, but her voice stops me.

"Konstantin," she says, and my name comes much more easily to her. "I wanted to ask...what is it you do, exactly?"

The one question I don't want to answer.

I look back at her, my gaze stony, and she seems to regret asking, so I soften my face as much as I can, to little avail. "Take a look at me, Rosie, and decide that for yourself."

Several minutes later, I'm out of the building and heading toward my car, not once looking back at the manor, as promised.

I must force the thoughts of Rosie out of my head as I pull out my cell phone. I know there's a part of me that doesn't want to go. I can't tell what exactly it is, but I feel such a strong sense of empathy with that woman in there that I want to make sure she is well cared for, no matter what. But I know the best thing I can do for her now is let her make her own choice. Besides, after what I've seen tonight, I suspect she's representative of a much larger problem that I plan to face head-on.

Looking at the text I received from the guard, I hit the 'call' button and listen to the phone ringing.

"...Mr. Alkaev? Hello?"

"Yes. Tell me, what is your name?"

"Dmitri, sir."

"Dmitri. How long have you served the Bratva?"

"...longer than I can remember, sir."

"So you've been a loyal *boekiv* through this recent power struggle. Good."

"Sir?"

"There are some rumors I need to follow up on if I am to assume this new role effectively. From now on, Dmitri, you do not answer to Anton. You answer to me. We need to meet, tonight — pick a bar. Once we're there, you will start by telling me everything you know about a peculiar man I've heard of associated with Brighton, a Siberian by the name of Andrei."

$\mathcal{I}$ lie here alone on the massive, California-king-size bed in the middle of this opulent room, my head still spinning with the overwhelming rush of events that I've recently lived through. I feel like Dorothy, like my whole life has been whirled away in a violent twister, leaving me stranded in this bizarre, Technicolor fantasy land. I'm definitely not in New Jersey anymore. This is Brighton Beach, and I no longer belong to myself.

I belong to him.

The tall, broad-shouldered, gorgeous, husky-voiced man who fucked me at gunpoint and then promptly whisked me away to this strange mansion. I didn't even know it was possible to own such a large, maze of a manor in this part of the state. Even when I lived in the depths of the antebellum South, I never saw such a magnificent, over-the-top house.

For a moment, I flash back to my warm, jasmine-scented memories of riding my little pink bicycle down the streets of a high-dollar neighborhood, staring in awe at the tall, beautifully-constructed pastel houses. They looked like real-life dollhouses, and I remember wondering if the people inside looked like the dolls I saw in the shop windows, but could never afford. It was a totally different world, a cold contrast to the tiny trailer I lived in back then.

Of course, once we moved up to New Jersey, I spent every night lying in bed wishing on every star in the sky that we could go back to Mississippi. Back to that little trailer decorated with dusty old finger-paintings and my mom's dying herbs and flowers, all curled stems and wilting petals. Because even though the light she once provided was totally snuffed out, at least in that trailer I still felt faint echoes of her presence. It was easier to feel close to her when we still lived in the same place she once lived.

Leaving Mississippi filled me with guilt. I remember watching the trailer park shrink away over the hill as we drove off toward the highway, thinking that we were leaving Mama behind, her ghost left alone and trapped down that dirt road.

Guilt fills my chest again now, as I bite my lip to keep from crying at the thought of Daisy and Sunny. I promised to protect them and keep them safe, swore that I would never leave them alone with our father. He's never hit them exactly, but he neglects them entirely, preferring to pretend they don't exist because their existence reminds him that his wife is gone.

It isn't their fault. I have screamed at him a hundred times to take pity on them, to love them as they dutifully, inexplicably love him. The girls are so sweet and innocent that they continue to strive for his affection, despite years and years of the most stubborn cold shoulder anyone has ever experienced. I sit up in bed and draw my legs up close to my chest, resting my chin on my knees and biting my lip hard, forcing myself to stay strong. Sitting here crying will definitely not help them, or me, for that matter.

I still can't figure out whether I'm in danger or not. I mean, judging by the events of yesterday, I have to assume I'm now neck-deep in trouble, thanks to the ever-constant fuck-ups of my father. At first, I was too blindsided by the whole situation to really consider why this was happening. But over time it has dawned on me that my dad's gambling addiction has finally taken complete and utter control over his life. Well, the gambling shares a throne with the drinking, of course. They're co-rulers of Frank Barnes's life. And I have become the most recent pay-off method. When credit cards reach their limits and the meager life savings have dried up, I suppose it makes sense that my dad would turn to the only other assets he's got left: his children.

I wince at the thought of my sisters finding the same fate, eventually.

Steeling myself, I resolve to never let that happen. I hope desperately that my father will have at least enough decency not to try and sell them off until they're of age. I know there are horrible, evil predators out there who *would* pay top-dollar for underaged little girls, and it fills my gut with roiling fury to think about.

But this man who has bought me…

The Bull. Konstantin Alkaev.

Neither of these names mean much to me, other than the fact that they're pretty intimidatingly foreign. His names certainly offer a fitting preview of what he's like. Huge, powerful, and a force of nature. But from my interactions with him, especially one on one, he is less like an angry bull in an arena and more like… well, an overly-cautious bull in a proverbial china shop. Like he is fully aware of how terrifying he is, and he wants to make certain I don't feel any fear toward him. It reminds me of the Disney movie I watched over and over again as a little girl, *The Beauty and the Beast.* To rescue my bumbling father, I have been swept away to this castle and held captive here by a beast of a man.

Only, I'm not exactly captive, am I?

I scan the room carefully, looking for hidden

cameras or something. It seems only natural that a man like Konstantin would have to trick out his mansion with state-of-the-art security. Then again, I get the profound sense that even he is out of context here. Like this isn't the way he wants to live and this whole mansion shebang has him totally out of his element. It's so lavishly decorated, the place looks more appropriate for a modern-day sheik than a strong, quiet man like the Bull. Even as he showed me around earlier, he seemed unhappy with his surroundings.

Maybe it's a rental, I reason, slightly amused at the thought of someone like Konstantin going through a realty company. It would be like watching a bear try to file taxes.

But I shake myself of these oddly warm thoughts. It's not like I know anything about him, really. All I really know are the facts:

He's a dangerous man, probably part of the mafia.

He bought me like I'm just some flashy new appliance.

And he stole my virginity at gunpoint.

Granted, it wasn't *his* gun aimed at us the entire time, but that little technicality does little to change the violent, horror-film nature of my first time. Still, though, I cannot fool myself into forgetting how bizarrely *good* it felt. How his hands on my body, his lips on mine, his massive cock inside me felt right.

No one has ever gotten close enough to make me feel anything like that. I have never allowed myself to be distracted away from my responsibilities with something as inconsequential and unnecessary as sex. But I find myself shivering a little at the memory of Konstantin's fingers deftly working my clit, toying my nipples, pulling at my hair and bringing me to an overwhelming, unexpected orgasm. I close my eyes and imagine his hard cock rubbing teasingly along the slick opening of my cunt, toying with me, making me want him more until I beg for him to release me from this awful frustration. I think about the way he felt inside me, filling my pussy so completely, stabbing into that deep, magical spot over and over until the pleasure is almost painful, it's so intense.

I lie back on the bed instinctively, my fingers trailing down between my thighs to lightly trace along the dampening spot in my panties, arching up into my own delicate touch until I'm moaning, Konstantin's gorgeous gray eyes piercing through my memory. I bite my lip and start to slip my fingers underneath the elastic band of my panties, when I suddenly jerk myself back to reality with a frustrated groan.

How can I be so silly? So selfish?

Touching myself to the memory of that horrible fuck-or-be-murdered scenario? What is wrong with me?! And more importantly, how can I possibly be useful to Daisy and Sunny while I'm still lounging around in this luxurious honeymoon suite?

I kick my legs over to the edge of the bed and slide down, looking around for something to wear. I'm still wearing just my leggings and bra, and I definitely cannot go out like this. It's strange, this place definitely doesn't seem to suit Konstantin at all. But why would he take me here if it isn't his home? Is this some kind of communal penthouse, shared by various members of the mafia? Just a lavish crash pad for a mobster and his most recent conquest, to bed down and shack up?

"Well," I murmur aloud as I start searching through a massive, vintage-looking armoire across the room, "I am nobody's conquest. And I am definitely not shacking up with you, Mister Alkaev. I got shit to do."

All of the clothes I find in the drawers are too small and sleazy-looking to belong to Konstantin. Like the man who lived here before was some kind of high-stakes Russian businessman or something. I see more gold velour, polyester, and silk than I would expect in a stripper's work locker. (Except, I imagine those fabrics work a whole lot better on a beautiful girl than on a probably paunchy, chain-smoking Moscow mobster.)

I pull out several lacy panties and skimpy thongs from the drawers, some of them obviously worn and then... not washed. I grimace and toss them aside, disgusted at the thought of some gross man hoarding women's used underwear. Now I hope more than ever that this place doesn't belong to Konstantin. So far, he's been bizarrely chivalrous in his behavior toward me, despite the horrific circumstances of our meeting. It would be totally incongruous with what I know of him to find out this mansion is really his. I can't imagine the Bull collecting used thongs and squeezing his obscene muscles into a stretchy, silvery pantsuit.

No. This has to be a shared facility.

A fortress or headquarters for the sleazy elite.

Either way, I have to get the hell out of here. After all, Konstantin made it very clear to me that he would understand if I left. Maybe he wants me to leave. He did say that his mission is to rescue and set free the girls captured and enslaved by the mafia. So perhaps this is just another step in the plan to get me out of trouble.

Then again, how can I even trust him? I don't know much about him other than my own instincts and the fact that he's involved with the mafia. For all I know, he could be totally on their side and simply playing me, testing me to see how loyal I am and how quickly I run off, only to re-capture me and bring me back here for punishment.

I gulp nervously at the prospect of what the mafia might consider an appropriate punishment for running away. If he is just another enforcer of the code, then perhaps there's a reason he's been so strangely gentle with me so far; he's just luring me into a false sense of security so that he can tear the rug out from underneath me later.

A terrifying thought.

Still, he was just so tender with me last night on the boat… so genuine in his concern for my comfort and wellbeing. He could have simply ravaged and abused my body, given the Mafioso onlookers a real show of violent masculinity by hurting me and disregarding my feelings, simply using me for his own pleasure. But instead, he seemed to really care, trying to make the whole ordeal as quick and painless as possible for me. How can he be that convincing of an actor?

Unless he's just got years and years of practice.

My stomach turns at the thought.

Maybe he's only good at this because this is his job. He's bedded a hundred girls at gunpoint, pretending to do it hesitantly, then showering them with tenderness to cushion the blow of what's really going on, earning their trust, only to turn around and become the bad guy when they least expect it!

I feel nauseous, my head dizzy and my heart pounding. To think I almost fell for it! To think… I could've caught something from him!

Quickly, I grab the plainest shirt I can find, which is still an oversized, silky button-up shirt probably stained with cheap vodka and bodily fluids, and put it on. I wrinkle my nose at the thought that some nasty mobster has worn this at some point, but I have to suck it up. The last thing I need is to draw attention to myself by walking out in a bra.

I spend the next few minutes anxiously standing at the door, listening intently to hear if there are any signs of life in the rest of the gigantic house. It was dark when Konstantin brought me here last night, so I'm worried that I might get lost or run into some hidden guard or trap on my way out. But I take a long, slow breath, reminding myself that I cannot let fear keep me trapped in this room. Not when I know Daisy and Sunny are back in New Jersey with only my father to care for them.

My heart aches, realizing how hungry they must be.

This thought gives me the spur of courage I need to slip out the door and tiptoe down a long hallway to the spiral staircase. I peer down over the banister and can't see anyone else down there, so I decide it's safe to keep going. As quietly as I can, I make my way down the stairs and into the magnificent foyer, glancing up at the sparkling chandelier hanging far above. The ceilings here are ridiculously high, and the whole place makes me feel dwarfed, even though I'm taller than average at about five-foot-six. It's not often that I feel small, but this place definitely gets the job done in that regard.

I sneak down a mirrored, grand hallway to the

front door, amazed that I've found my way back so easily, without running into anyone. But then I recall that Konstantin dismissed the guards last night, as though he expected this. Like he knew I would leave.

I feel a surge of panic at this realization, that he has so perfectly predicted my intentions.

But regardless of the outcome, I have to try. I have to escape. If not for my sake, then for the love of my innocent little sisters. They need me.

So I cautiously unlock the five different padlocks on the front door and slip out into the early morning sunshine, blinking in the light. I take a deep breath of free air — and then bolt for the road. The grounds aren't anywhere near as elaborate as the inside of the mansion, with overgrown bushes and weeds everywhere. Still, I am relieved to find that there isn't a gate or anything — I can just walk right out of the compound and onto the main road. I take off toward what I hope is the city center of Brighton Beach, thinking maybe I can find some way to hitch-hike back to Jersey or something. People hardly seem to notice me, even in my oversized black silk shirt and slightly disheveled appearance, as though the folks of Brighton Beach have all seen much worse.

I follow the signs and my instincts almost all the way to the bus station, where I hope I can somehow finagle or panhandle my way to a one-way ticket. But as I stand there on the sidewalk, I am suddenly overcome with a strange, overwhelming sense that I'm doing the wrong thing. I've made a huge mistake.

I remember the apology, the genuine regret in Konstantin's beautiful eyes as he made love to me on the boat. The way he held me, cradled in his arms, his lips soft on mine. A shiver of fear rustles through me. Perhaps he really was trying to help me.

Or is he just simply a fantastic actor, well-versed in the art of seducing and deceiving young women? This has to be a trick of some kind. A test. To see if I'm worth keeping or... possibly just discarded. Maybe it's a hazing ritual: giving me the glimmer of freedom only to have it heartlessly ripped away.

Despite the pull back toward home, back to my little sisters who need me, I have to think straight and face the reality that I really, truly do not know enough about my captor to reasonably assume he will even let me make it home. He could be watching me right now, following my every move to see what I do next. The move I make from here could determine whether I live or die. I've only been thinking of Daisy and Sunny, worrying that I have to get back to them.

But what if that's what he wants? To watch me, and let me lead him back to my family.

No. I can't risk it. And it's not like I even have a penny on me to pay for the bus anyhow.

I stand on the curb, conflicted, watching the cars zoom by and the buses arrive at the station just down the block. I bite my lip and wonder if I should take this possible olive branch and run… or just face the music here in Brighton Beach. I have the distinct feeling of being caught in a trap with an unwinnable game laid out before me. Do I wait for the hunter to release me from the snare, or do I chew off my own leg to escape?

"And you're sure he'll agree to meet?" I ask.

"Nothing is sure, sir, I'll admit. He's a man who often lays low now. But something like what we've stumbled on might be the thing to get him back onto the radar, if anything will. Even after all this time, he's elusive, so a shot in the dark is as good as anything."

"I see. Thank you, Dmitri. I won't forget this."

"Don't mention it," Dmitri says as I lay down a wad of cash to pay for our drinks, the smoke-filled bar's patrons starting to trickle out as closing time rolls past. "I didn't join up for things like what I saw take place on that yacht. I'm glad to see someone in charge who won't tolerate it either."

I raise my eyebrows, finishing off my drink. "Don't praise a fish for swimming, Dmitri. We have a lot of work ahead of us yet."

Dmitri nods, and we stand up, heading out of the bar. He takes a deep breath as we leave the thick air behind us, and he looks at me as I start heading towards my car. "Anyway, what happened to that young woman who was with you? Where is she now?"

I glance back at him, a frown on my face. "That, I look forward to finding out shortly."

Understanding, the man gives a wave. "Take care, boss." Moments later, I'm back in my car, driving down the thinly-populated roads back to the manor.

In hindsight, leaving Rosie alone at the manor might have been an oversight. There was still much uncertainty surrounding the place and those who would be frequenting it. There's been so much confusion and haste tonight that it was the best option, though. Bringing her with me would have been too much for her to bear, and dropping her off somewhere else would have been even riskier.

Nevertheless, as I pull up the manor's driveway — my own driveway, now — I can't help but wonder whether there would be anyone inside upon my arrival.

The house is quiet when I push the door open. As I do, my heart sinks as I realize the door is unlocked. The door has many padlocks from the inside, but only one on the outside that I'd locked on my way out, and she didn't have the key. If the door is unlocked now, that can mean only one thing — she left the house. She must have taken my offer and headed for the nearest public transport she could find.

I step into the silent house, and I feel a mix of emotions. To my surprise, the first is merely guilt that I didn't leave her money to pay her way home, but I suppose there's some money to be found lying around the property that she might have had time to take. But maybe I should have encouraged her to stay longer, let me help her get back on her feet from...whatever she went through before me. Maybe I should have warned her that it would be safer here. Maybe I should have kept her company for the night, at least.

Or maybe I was just thinking of excuses so that I'd enjoy her a little longer.

But it was the right thing to do, in the long run, I decide as I head down the hallway on the ground floor. She's an adult, if only barely so, and restoring her independence had to be the first thing I did with her under my care. My first few weeks as the leader of Brighton's Bratva will be marred by blood and fear, and I cannot force her to go through all that against her will, regardless of the fact that she may be the closest thing to a friend I have right now, aside from Dmitri.

I step into the kitchen, wondering if the men guarding the place have left anything around to eat. Beer and bar popcorn was an unusual introduction to American fare, but I tell myself I'll stock the house with some more suitable Russian food tomorrow morning.

Once I'm inside, though, an orange glow catches my eye. I glance at the stove and notice one of the burners still red-hot from use, but all the dials are off. Instinctively, my hand goes to my concealed gun, and I spin around at the sound of a little gasp.

And I freeze at the sight of a terrified Rosie holding a cup of freshly brewed tea in her hand, leaning back against the counter.

We stare at each other in silence for a moment before she tentatively holds her cup out to me. "...did...you want some?"

My hand leaves my gun, and I let myself laugh a little, even as she only manages a faint smile.

"I apologize," I say, rubbing the back of my neck and letting my hand slip around to my tired eyes. "I thought you were gone, and my reflexes, they..." I start to say that it's been a long night, but it seems like an insulting thing to say to a woman who was recently forced to have sex with me, so I fall silent.

"It's okay," she says, "I'm kind of surprised I'm still here too, to be honest. I'm just glad you weren't one of the guards coming back for something." My eye catches the kitchen knife on the counter near her for the first time, and I raise my eyebrow as she moves to obstruct my view of it with a sheepish look in her eye.

"Do you know how to use something like that?" I ask, crossing my arms, and she frowns.

"Well, unless it's some vegetables or a pork chop try to break into the house, not really," she confesses. She's silent a moment longer before raising her eyes to mine. "How did your 'calls' go? Learn anything worthwhile?"

My eyes haven't left her since I stepped into the kitchen. She has impressive resilience to still be here. If the door was unlocked when I left, that means that she *did* go through the door, but she must have come back inside. She did indeed leave, but something brought her back, of her own free will. *What, though?*

"It went well," I finally say. "I've only been to America once or twice before now, so there is a lot to get a hold of as I get settled in here."

"Brighton does seem nice," she says to my surprise, crossing her arms over her stomach and looking out the kitchen window. "Nice views, hopping nightlife, perfect place for clandestine meetings and mafia plotting, huh?" She offers a smile at her own joke, and I return it, starting to catch on.

One does not go far in my line of work without gaining a sharp ability to read people in any situation. Knowing the difference between a coward and a desperate man or between a bluster and a sincere threat is essential to evaluating targets and threats. And that skill helps me understand what Rosie seems to be doing now.

She's been pushed to her limits tonight, but even so, she's trying to make light of the situation after I nearly pulled a gun on her. She's the kind of person to try to make a joke to her captor, which is what I know she still sees me as, despite her willing return. A less attentive eye might dismiss the behavior as merely being cocky, but I recognize the coping mechanism. She probably comes from a rough household. Trying to appease an abuser no matter what is not something that comes naturally to any personality, it is something that is learned. And in her case and at her age, it's probably a honed skill.

It's also a shame to realize that she feels the need to use it with me, but I don't question her.

"If you think New York is a good place for that, you should see Moscow," I say, turning to rummage through the pantry and finding what seems to be some packets of crackers with cheese and tearing into them. "But there are some good people here."

"Oh, I'm sure," she says, feigning sincerity rather well. I make quick work of the food. I notice an empty pizza box at her side on the counter — she probably finished off whatever the guards had for dinner.

"I'll tell you more in the morning," I say, deciding that she's had enough to process for tonight. "Head on upstairs, I'm going to get something for you."

A few minutes later, after I run back out to my car and come back, I push open the bedroom door to find Rosie sitting on the bed with the sheets over her legs. "Are you sure you don't want this bed for tonight?" she says in greeting, setting her now empty cup aside.

"Quite," I say, regarding the gaudy bed again. "I'm used to more...simple accommodations."

"Well, we have that in common," she says, "but I'll take what I can get." Her eyes fall on the laptop that I now have in my hands, and I step to her side to lay it on the mattress.

"I thought you'd need something to occupy your mind in the morning," I say, reaching into my wallet and rifling through it while she blinks at me, confused. "So I'm going to leave my laptop with you. I don't use it for work, so feel free to do with it what you will." I pull out what I was looking for — a sleek credit card, which I set on top of the laptop, and I watch her eyes widen further. "There's no limit on that. Take me on my word when I say that money is no issue with me, Rosie. Feel free to buy a few things for yourself in the morning."

She appears to be speechless, confirming what I suspected about her background. In truth, I just don't know how else to try to make her comfortable, so I suppose letting her decide that for herself is the best way to go about things.

"I'm going to be meeting with someone in the morning, out of the house, so I'm going to get some sleep. Is there something else I can get for you?"

Rosie blinks a few times, then looks up at me with a half-smile. "After giving me free access to the outside world and more money than I've ever thought of in my whole life? I don't know, a glass of water?"

I smile at the request as she pulls the covers a little higher over her, and I head out the door, slipping my jacket off. I know it to be a joke. But it's worth the walk downstairs to see the look on her face when I come back a few minutes later with an actual glass of water.

"Oh! Oh my god, I didn't actually mean-"

"It's okay, Rosie," I say, offering a smile. "I can't sleep without it either, personally. You've more than earned a comfortable night's rest. Me, I could go another day or so without sleep."

She smiles at me, and this time, I can tell that it's sincere, at least in part, and that's enough to satisfy me. "I...really appreciate it, Konstantin," she says. There's a pause. "So, I won't ask again, but if I'm going to be staying with you for a while, I just wanted to ask — I can look at you and guess a hundred different things you might do for the other Russians around here, but..."

I can sense her question, and my smile fades, even if I know I owe her an answer. Finally, I nod. "I carry out the will of the Bratva or my clients, Rosie, through quick, precise action. I earn my living by being given targets, and I do what needs to be done."

I look her in the eye, those sapphire eyes that seem to have their fear again fanned in them every bit as fiercely as I'd worried.

"In your tongue, I'm called a hitman."

I'M USED to five or six hours of sleep per day, and this morning was no different. I sit at an outdoor table at a small cafe in Brighton Beach proper, pretending to thumb through some book on a Kindle.

This is the place Dmitri said he'd try to arrange as a point of contact for me and this Andrei. Among other things, it was revealed to me that the man in question is almost singlehandedly responsible for Sergei Slokavich's death, meaning that he's partially responsible for my presence here. I find it only fitting that I have a word with him myself. But it all rides on whether or not he'll show.

An hour passes, and I've ordered a coffee to keep the staff from eyeballing me disdainfully. I start to suspect that today will be a no-show. In any case, I suppose, it will be good to scout out the city I'm supposed to be in charge of.

This was not going to be an easy transition. The similarities between assassination and leading the local Bratva are scarce, save that I'll be using my people skills and keeping eyes and ears everywhere.

From now on, I realize, the contracts I take will have to be more measured. More precise. So the more hidden assets I have, I suppose, the better.

And just when I'm ready to pay my bill and leave, the potential asset I've been waiting on all morning strides up to my table and takes a seat without a word.

Andrei is hard to miss. He's as large as I am, with a look that only the Siberian winter can breed. Where I'm wearing a tight-fitting tank top and jeans, my Bratva star showing proudly on my muscled chest, he wears a dark leather jacket, the collar on it pulled high. I turn to face him as he regards me, and we size each other up for a moment before he speaks to me in Russian.

"So you're the one they call The Bull."

"I'm in Brighton one day, but my reputation preceded me?" I ask, raising an eyebrow.

"You were an interesting choice to replace the last *pakhan*," Andrei says, leaning back in his chair, "who happened to be a man I worked very hard to remove. I did a little homework on you as soon as Dmitri said you wished to meet. Have to make sure I'm not walking in on my own assassination," he says with the faintest hint of a smile.

"Oh?" I say, folding my hands behind my head, "I'm interested in what you learned, then."

"I learned your reputation started before you earned that red star behind bars," he says, nodding to my chest. "Your time in the Spetznaz didn't end on good terms, but the fact that you weren't executed led to even more interesting leads surrounding the details of your discharge. Some would call you a traitor, you know," he says, and I flex my fist.

"Some? Would you?"

"Me, I'm a man who's borne that same title," he says, stripping his jacket off at last. "And it may be self-serving to say, but traitors are some of the best people I've ever met."

I grin, and at last we extend hands to shake firmly. "Then it's a pleasure to meet you, Andrei."

"And you, Konstantin Alkaev. I think we could have a lot to reflect on together, but I assume you haven't set this rendezvous up for small talk, have you?"

I wave off the waitress as I shake my head at Andrei and spend the next few minutes filling him in on the events leading up to what brings me to the table with him this morning, and the other assassin listens with the same attention to detail that I would.

"I have heard much about your work through Dmitri. How you carried out a string of assassinations and brought the Bratva's flourishing slave trade to its knees. And I believe," I say after finishing my account, "that I was brought here to be manipulated while whatever remnants of that slave ring tries to recuperate itself. I'm strong enough that nobody could challenge me, but they want to pressure me into letting them rebuild. What happened on that yacht was a message."

"No doubt," Andrei says, his hands steepled in front of him. "But something doesn't fit. When I rooted out the slave ring, I was thorough. The Bratva should have been cleansed of this filth."

"Maybe," I say, "but here we are."

Andrei nods, his frown deep. Then he looks back up at me. "I'm surprised that you're here, frankly. Those who gave you this position did so because they thought you could be played, maybe over-whelmed by the new responsibilities."

"Many who are born into poverty and later given the world on a silver platter are often wooed into doing great evils," I say, crossing my legs, "but I cannot ignore the hardship I faced when I was young. I'm in a position to finalize the changes you strove for in the Bratva, really change things for the better. But I can't do that as long as my subordinates think it's acceptable to get away with carrying on the slave trade." Andrei nods, and I lean forward, looking him in the eye. "Andrei, I want you to help me put this to rest, once and for all. Cleanse the Bratva of this filth. I need someone who's been on the inside to root it out."

The man across the table from me gives a solemn nod. "It will be done. And if we succeed, I'll be proud to call you *pakhan*." He grins and adds, "Though the American-born locals might be more apt to call you

'Godfather.' In any case, I think I know what could solve our problem in one fell swoop. But it will take time. And it will take money — more than either of us have, I can tell you that much."

I nod, expecting him to continue. "And if you're proposing this, I suspect you have a means of bringing in this kind of money?"

Andrei narrows his eyes. "You could say I've had my eye on a job."

$\mathcal{I}$ have never known what it's like to have money.

Even back in my sunniest, most carefree childhood memories, wealth was never a factor in my happiness. I have known love and joy, but never fortune. We lived in a rundown trailer park, for god's sake. Years before my father's gambling addiction and alcoholism catapulted us into neck-deep debt, we struggled to make ends meet, both my parents toiling away with whatever they could possibly manage. Granted, I was a young child then, and that life was all I'd ever known. So I was more or less oblivious to how impoverished we really were, how close to the very edge we lived.

So when Konstantin tossed a limitless credit card my way and told me to use it however I wanted, it took a long time for my brain to even compute his words into something comprehensible. For all my life, I never even knew people could own limitless credit cards. In fact, I tend to view all credit cards with suspicion and distrust, since my father has maxed out card after card in his pursuit of booze and blackjack, plummeting us even further into debt.

At first, I assumed Konstantin was either playing a cruel joke on me or just testing me to see how gullible or greedy I am. Maybe he wants to gauge whether I can be distracted by pretty, shiny things, caught off-guard while entranced by the glittering mirage of consumerism.

Or perhaps he really does feel guilty for buying me, and he's trying to make it up to me by offering me money and gifts. He wants to appease me, prove that he's not the monster his background builds him up to be. But I also get the sense that he doesn't quite know what kinds of things I would even like. To be fair, *I* hardly know what I like.

My life for the past eight years has never been about what I like, what I want, need, or aspire to. Ever since Daisy and Sunny were born and my mother passed away, my life has centered entirely around taking care of them. From the moment I first named them and held them in my arms, it was clear that life as I knew it was totally over. It wasn't about goofing around in the woods, looking forward to birthday presents, or getting attention from my parents anymore. It was about changing diapers and staying up all night and doing whatever I had to in order to keep us all alive.

Sometimes I wonder how different I would be if things had turned out differently — if my mom was still alive and my dad had never lost his mind. Who would I be without the weight of the world on my shoulders?

I shift uncomfortably in bed, crossing my ankles under the sheet and sipping my glass of water thoughtfully. I should know better by now than to dwell on pointless 'what ifs' like that. Especially when there are present-day, real-life problems popping up to screw with me every five minutes. For instance, right now I need to determine how the hell I'm going to look out for my sisters while I'm holed up in this mansion, not even in the same state.

I shudder to think of how terrible the past day or so has been for them. Without me around, who will care for them? Who will make sure they have food?

Luckily, I have done a pretty thorough job of preparing them for all kinds of awful situations. They know how to call 9-1-1. They know the number for child protective services. They know not to disobey or anger Dad whenever he's in a bad mood — which is just about all the time nowadays. I even printed out a map of the area for them while I was at the public library one time, going over the streets and various important locations. I circled our address, along with the locations of the police station, fire station, bus station, grocery store, and homeless shelter, just in case. I spent hours grilling them on how they should act under different circumstances, such as if anything were to happen to them while I'm gone.

One good thing about our current living situation is the fact that there is a sweet, elderly woman three houses down who is always more than willing to look after the girls if I ever need to go somewhere without them. She was a godsend last summer when I had to work long hours as a waitress and didn't want to leave Sunny and Daisy at home with my dad while I was working. Of course, Ms. Liddell is quite old and frail, so she would not be a great caretaker for most children. But my sisters are well-trained from years of having to be quiet, soft, and polite in order to escape our father's violent temper. They love to help Ms. Liddell tend to her garden, bake cookies, make lemonade, and other simple little tasks. Most evenings when I came to collect them after work, I would find all three of them snuggled up in their respective armchairs, game show reruns playing on the ancient television set.

I hope that's where they are now — hunkered down at Ms. Liddell's house watching TV, far from my father's destructive reach. At least if they're with her, they will have something to eat and a place to sleep without having to worry about Frank Barnes thundering into the house in the middle of the night in a drunken stupor. Sure, I would never expect Ms. Liddell to allow them to stay with her indefinitely, especially since she's got to be pushing eighty years old and the last thing she needs is to become a mother figure to two very energetic, precocious twin girls. But I like to think that in a way, it's a mutually beneficial dynamic, since the girls are always so willing and enthusiastic about helping her around the house.

I try to assure myself that they're definitely with her right now; that they're safe and sound at Ms. Liddell's house, and I need not worry. But I know there is still a chance that they could just be at home, starving and shivering in fear because their big sister, the closest thing to a mother they have ever known, is gone.

I have to blink several times and bite the inside of my cheek to stem the flow of tears threatening to spill out. I can't let this break me. I'm stronger than this. There is nothing I can do about the situation outside this mansion, no way for me to check in on the girls, so I might as well take my mind off of it somehow. It isn't helpful to anyone for me to lose my mind over something beyond my control.

But it's difficult to distract myself from my thoughts. Unless…

I glance down at the credit card laid out on the end table on my side of the bed, its holographic gold face lightly shimmering in the early morning light. To my right is a sleek silver laptop, fully charged and ready for use. I have to admit that it is a little endearing to have such a big, powerful man seemingly doing his very best to provide me with creature comforts.

I have never even owned a computer, myself, because we simply never had the money. I know how to use, of course, after painstakingly teaching myself how to use the public access computers at the library back in Mississippi. In school, they taught us how to type, but it was up to me to learn how to use the Internet, how to apply for jobs and send emails. With a glittery golden credit card on my left and a shiny silver laptop on my right, I feel quite literally surrounded by luxury. This is not a world I have much experience with. In fact, the last time I can remember spending any frivolous money on myself was when I used some of my waitressing tips to get my nose pierced. I bought the cheapest, smallest little stud they had available, and even then I refused to eat anything but dollar-store bread and lettuce for a few days to make up for my purchase.

Running a finger delicately over the little nose stud, I remember how angry my father was once he finally noticed the piercing. It took him a week to notice. I wince at the memory of his double take, the color fading from his cheeks as he turned white with rage and his hands curled into fists. He had been so angry with me, so offended that any daughter of his would "do something so filthy and trashy to her body."

After scrimping and saving for months to afford this one small luxury for myself, I was devastated at my father's over-the-top reaction. In fact, before I could stop myself, I had angrily muttered in response, "Right, because drinking yourself to death is much classier than getting your nose pierced."

It was the first time my dad hit me so hard I had to get medical help.

Thankfully, it took place over the summer so nobody at school got to see me with a black eye and bloody lip. After Dad threw a few rapid punches my way, I calmly left and walked all the way to the nearest clinic, where a nurse took pity on me and gave me a massive discount on an ice pack and some pain medication. She mopped up the blood, dried my tears, and begged me to let her call child protective services. But I knew that if CPS came, there was a good chance I would end up separated from my little sisters, and that was a fate I just could not abide. So I thanked her, paid her with every last meager cent from my little thrift store wallet, and walked back home to face the music.

Luckily, my dad was so drunk by the time I got home, he had completely forgotten the whole incident, and the twins were still at Ms. Liddell's house for the night. I simply blamed my black eye on my nose piercing, telling Daisy and Sunny that it was a freak reaction, a rare side effect of having someone jab a needle through my nose, but that it totally didn't hurt and was nothing for them to worry about.

My father, thank god, never mentioned it again.

I paid so dearly for that one small gift to myself, a reward for managing to juggle all the endless responsibilities I am saddled with. And now, I have the power to buy myself nearly anything I want, and I'm sitting here reminiscing sadly about the past.

For once, I'm going to get what I want, at least in some small, frivolous way. Besides, I think to myself as I open the laptop and drop the credit card in my lap, online shopping is probably a good way to distract myself from my troubles.

I open Amazon and start shyly perusing the more practical categories of home goods, looking at different colors of towels and dishes. Then I remind myself that there is really no need for anything like that here. This mansion has all the essentials in it already. I look around the room, wrinkling my nose. Everything here is lavish and extravagant, but it's also… sleazy.

The place looks like it was decorated by a megalomaniacal Russian nightclub owner or something, and it definitely does not suit my tastes. Even the bed sheets pulled up to my waist are an overly slick gold color, more fitting as a circus tent tarp than a blanket. I quickly order a new set of sheets and pillowcases patterned with phases of the moon in gray and white. The whole thing costs nearly two hundred dollars, and my heart races as I enter the credit card information and press submit. To my amazement, the purchase goes through successfully.

It's the most money I have ever spent at one time. In fact, two hundred dollars is generally enough to last the girls and me for a few months of groceries and necessities.

I feel slightly invigorated, and a little bit nauseous. But Konstantin did tell me to buy whatever I wanted, anything to make me feel a little more at home. So I go on to purchase several vintage-looking T-shirts with classic rock band logos on them, three pairs of jeans in what I hope is my size, a pair of black ankle boots, a black faux-leather jacket, a black felt hat, a couple of plaid flannel shirts, some socks, and a long, slinky dark red dress. It's strange, seeing the Amazon cart filled with so much clothing that all seems to go together. I smile to myself, surprised to see that maybe I do have a sense of style all my own, after all. It's remarkable how put-together a person can look when there's enough money involved.

"What will it be like to have more than one pair of pants?" I murmur aloud, admittedly a little giddy at the prospect of having a somewhat complete wardrobe for the first time in my life. There's still a persistent pang of guilt beating at my heart, but I force myself to ignore it in the name of distracting myself from worry.

By the time Konstantin returns around mid-morning, I am downright effervescent with consumerist high. I can hear his key in the front door from across the silent house, and I quickly shut the laptop and push it away from me as though I have to hide my shameful purchases. Even though he was the one who urged me to make them in the first place. It hits me now just how awful it is that shame and fear are my default emotions. I have been so intensely, rigorously programmed to conceal my needs and desires, to hide my soul away lest my father comes home to destroy anything left out in plain sight.

The Bull knocks gently on my bedroom door and I clear my throat to call out, "Oh — come in! I'm in bed but I-I'm decent." The words sound flimsy and needless once I remember that we have already had sex. He's already seen me naked. Nothing he could find in this room would come as a surprise to him.

Still, I do appreciate his gentlemanly knock, as well as the way he averts his eyes when he walks into the room. He stands tall and solemn, his eyes cast across the room toward the window. Morning light streams in through the blinds, softly illuminating his handsome features. Somehow, he manages to look simultaneously intimidating and gentle, his serene expression barely even hinting at the power he keeps hidden away inside. Like gray clouds gathering overhead just before a storm. He is a fenced-in danger, a rabid dog kept on a tight leash.

I gulp.

"How did you sleep?" he asks in that thrumming baritone.

"Good," I lie. Actually, I tossed and turned for a few hours, my mind racing.

"Did you use the credit card I gave you?" he continues.

"Y-yes. I hope that's okay," I reply sheepishly. "I promise I didn't buy anything too ridiculous."

"You can have anything you want," Konstantin says meaningfully, turning to look at me. His gray eyes seem to pierce right through me, sending a cold shiver down my spine.

"Where did you go?" I ask suddenly, before I can think better of it.

He pauses for a moment, then to my surprise, he says, "I contacted an old ally of mine and we discussed a plan to clear out some of the filth clogging up the Bratva."

"The slavers?" I ask, sitting up straighter. "Fuck them. I want to take them down."

Konstantin raises one eyebrow, clearly taken aback by my outburst. I blush.

"I mean… they are the ones who did this to me," I explain, "and knowing that there are other girls out there in much worse conditions… I just — I want to help you. However I can."

There is a long moment of silence, and Konstantin appears to be ruminating over my admission. I am worried at first that he will either laugh at me or be angry, but instead he simply replies, "We have an idea in mind to bring in the kind of money required for our plan, but it would require one hell of a distraction to pull it off."

"Distraction?" I question, cocking my head to one side.

Konstantin nods, the faintest twitch of a smile on his lips.

My suit is gunmetal-gray, a black shirt underneath it unbuttoned at the top, showing the peak of my chest as the buttons keep it closed snugly over my rippling muscles. There's more stubble on my face than usual — I've neglected the razor in the past couple of days' planning.

I'm pacing around the living room when Rosie finally steps out of my room in her outfit, and when I turn to look at her, I nearly lose my breath at the beauty before me. Rosie is naturally a gorgeous woman, but she's outdone herself tonight. The evening dress she's wearing spills down her form like a dark scarlet waterfall, ending at her knees, hanging elegantly off her shoulders and hugging her breasts and hips as though it were made for her. It contrasts with her pale skin in a way that makes me want to tear her out of the dress and forget our whole plan in a rush of passion.

I've been a gentleman with her, though. Even though I catch those glances of her, and there's some instinct in me that tells me she feels the same.

Whether she's forgiven me or not for how we met, over the past couple of days I have noticed that her defensive snark has begun to fade, replaced instead with something bordering on carefree. It's taken us both by surprise.

I take her hand as she emerges, placing a hand around her waist. "Rosie, you look spectacular," I say, trying to mind my accent as I pronounce the word, and she smiles at my deep voice's effort.

"You're one to talk," she says, looking me up and down. "I didn't know they trained hitmen how to dress."

"You have to learn a thing or two about blending in with high society," I say, taking her by the arm as we turn to leave. "When the rich and powerful are your targets, you must be able to blend in with them." She seems to think about that curiously for a moment, a faint smile on her lips, and I add, "Are you ready for tonight?"

Her blue eyes look back up to me, playful light in them. "Ready to take part in a multi-million dollar heist in a place I've never even heard of when the most acting I've ever done was *Midsummer Night's Dream* in high school? Sure, yeah."

Chuckling, I lead her out of the house and to my car, where we get in and start driving to our destination.

"This hotel is a five-star venue," I explain as we drive. "Very high society of Manhattan. What is the phrase you Americans use — upper bread?"

She blinks before stifling a laugh, shaking her head. "Upper *crust* is what you're thinking of. I hope."

I feel a little color in my cheeks, and I grin. "Not my fault American expressions are strange. In any case, let's recap."

Rosie nods, paying close attention to the plan I'd already gone over with her at least a dozen times. "There's a man staying at this hotel by the name of Montgomery Morrison. He's officially a jeweler, but he has extraordinarily deep pockets in the international jewel trade, and there's more than a little blood on his hand. Smuggling. Blood diamonds. Extortion. He's not above anything, and he's made more than a few enemies along the way. Someone has paid for Morrison's assassination, and our friend Andrei has set me up with the contract."

Rosie interjects, "And that's the contract you're going to...carry out. You're going to kill Morrison tonight." She says the words carefully, as though intimidated by their very pronunciation. I nod in response.

"Yes. It's something that will do a lot of good for many people in the big picture, Rosie."

"And the small picture," she says, looking at me confidently, to my surprise. "You're right. Don't worry, I won't be losing sleep over some slimy bastard."

I smile and proceed. "Morrison is my target for tonight, but he's the secondary target. He's carrying with him a case containing extraordinarily rare jewels, his latest acquisitions from a lucrative venture on the Gold Coast. There's a lot of blood those stones represent, but if Morrison gets away with them, they'll just be used to line his pockets. While I see to the assassination, Andrei takes care of acquiring the jewels from his hotel room. We can't undo the evil they represent, but we can put the money they're worth to good use. Andrei is already getting into position, so we won't be in contact with him for the duration of the night. We'll meet up after everything's said and done, at our manor."

Rosie smiles a bit at the words 'our manor,' and she nods. "So, you kill the bad guy and Andrei makes off with the jewels. And meanwhile-"

"Meanwhile," I pick up for her, "you'll be the distraction for the one real threat to this heist: Diego Milani, Morrison's personal attack dog. He's one of the top hitmen for the Italian mafia in New York City, and that is no small compliment. But he takes contract jobs like me and Andrei, so for tonight, he's working as a bodyguard."

"So I'm distracting a trained killer with a reputation in the local mafia," Rosie says, a nervous smile on her face, and I reach over to stroke her arm.

"Are you sure you can do this? You don't have to, if you don't want to."

"No, I want this," she says, and suddenly her voice exudes confidence again, and I nod.

"Very well. We considered including Diego in the hit, but that might start a war with the Italians that we don't want to tangle with right now. Fortunately, like any self-respecting Italian man, Diego has a weakness for women. And you, Rosie, are more woman than he'll be able to resist," I say, looking Rosie up and down. She smiles, squirming a little in her seat, checking her red lipstick in the mirror.

"I'm a regular femme fatale," she muses softly, half-joking. "You sure I won't look a little suspicious, coming up to him like that?"

"Andrei and I have read up on Diego," I say, "he won't ask questions. Just keep him distracted long enough that Morrison will go on a bathroom break. That's all I'll need. He's a drinker, so expect to find him with his bodyguard at the hotel bar. I've made a reservation at the hotel, so I'll be 'checking in' while you tend to Diego."

She takes a deep breath and nods. "What if things go wrong?"

"I'll extract you. Don't worry. I'll send you a text after the job is done, and you'll excuse yourself to meet me in the parking lot. After Morrison drops, our part is done, and we'll be out of the area within minutes. Diego is being paid well, but he has nothing personal in this. But just to make sure you're not in any danger," I say, reaching over to tap Rosie's purse, "I've installed a wire in your purse. It's hooked up to an earpiece I'll have in, meaning that I'll be able to hear your entire conversation with Diego. If there's trouble, I'll be there."

Rosie fingers her purse a little, nodding silently. She recites the whole plan back to me as we drive, the busy Manhattan traffic slowing our progress only a little as we make our way to the hotel.

At long last, we pull up into the driveway, and Rosie's eyes widen at the opulence before us. A fountain that seems to shimmer with golden light stands in front of the high doorways, and the building rises many, many stories high, gleaming in the spotlights with white marble. Golden lion statues stand outside the doors, and a red carpet leads indoors. I park the car and help Rosie out, and I can feel her heartbeat racing as I take her soft hand in my larger one. I look her in the eye again, a soft smile on my hard face. "You can do this, Rosie. I believe in you."

She looks up at me and seems to calm a little, giving a careful nod. "Not many people do." She forces a smile to her lips. "Let's see if your trust is well-placed, shall we? It's showtime."

Confidently, Rosie and I stride into the building, the doorman giving us a courteous nod as we enter. The interior seems to shimmer with wealth, a golden hue about the whole place. Soft piano music greets us as I watch Rosie's gaze look up to the high ceiling and enormous chandelier. It's like a more lively version of the manor — better staffed and bustling with activity.

"There's a show opening on Broadway tonight," I whisper to Rosie as we walk down the black tile floors to the desk. "Crowds from all over the world here."

I can see on Rosie's lips the desire to talk about how she's never seen anything like this, never pictured herself surrounded by so much wealth and affluence in one place, but she holds her tongue for now. She knows she has a part to play, and I'm impressed by how seamlessly she seems able to slip into the role.

"Ooh, we should go and see it!" she says in a normal speaking voice, putting on a starry-eyed face as she looks up to me. "You promised me a good time in New York, darling."

"We'll see, my dear," I say to her with a candid smile. "Why don't you go enjoy a drink while I get us checked in?"

Rosie stretches up to me, and I lean down to let

her peck me on the cheek, smiling as she turns to stride off to the hotel bar, her hips swaying as she makes her way down the hallway.

I've already shown her a picture of Morrison, so she knows who to target. I don't imagine there will be more than one towering Italian standing near that wretched bag of bones. Nonetheless, it makes me nervous to see Rosie go out of my sight so quickly, and I put in my earpiece when it doesn't seem like anyone is watching me before I make my way to the desk and start chatting up the receptionist.

I'm only half paying attention to the conversation I'm conducting with the receptionist as I hear Rosie's voice over the earpiece.

"Give me a martini, something sweet. If you can work a cherry into it, that'd be lovely," she says, her voice smooth as silk. I have to admit, her candor tonight has been remarkably composed, for someone who's never done this before. I don't want to tell her just yet, but she's a natural at this. I wonder how many times she's been forced to play the actress in some capacity in her life.

There is a tragic beauty surrounding so much about Rosie. I just want to give her the happiness she deserves so that she doesn't have to wear so many masks. If only it were possible already. But for now, we have a job to carry out.

As the receptionist in front of me starts typing away at his computer, to find the fake name I gave, I listen to the voice on my earpiece, and I can hear the bartender saying something.

"Ma'am, that martini has another one coming after it, courtesy of the gentleman down the bar."

"Oh?" There's a teasing lilt to her voice, and I can almost see her glancing down the bar. If there's another man besides Diego making a move on her, there could be trouble. I wait with baited breath as I hear her footsteps resume.

"I hope I wasn't too forward," I hear a voice in an Italian accent say as I let loose a breath of relief, "but it breaks my heart to see a woman drinking alone."

"You're too kind," Rosie says, and I'm astounded at the finesse in her voice. She sounds appreciative, but not so much as to make him suspect she's just fishing for more drinks. There's a vague disinterest tinged with the hint of something more in her tone. I'd be caught in her net myself, if I were in Diego's position.

"So tell me, what brings a lovely soul like you to Manhattan?" says Diego, and I can hear his voice closer as he leans in. "I'm no local, but I've been here long enough to be able to show strangers around."

I smile, bemused. *Italians.* The receptionist finishes checking me in, and I stride away from the desk with my room key, making my way to the bathroom near the bar to occupy a stall and take a seat. As I listen to Diego and Rosie engage in flirtatious small talk, I pull out my phone and navigate to a live camera feed Andrei and I had installed the day before.

We'd arranged nothing complicated. From here, I can monitor the feed from the security cameras in the hallway outside the hotel bar, leading to the bathroom. This should be all I need to watch Morrison make his way in. All there is to do now is play the waiting game. My hand drifts to the pistol strapped to my side, a force of habit.

Rosie keeps Diego talking, and I find myself smiling at the story she feeds him. She's passing herself off as a sugar baby to some old rich man who's losing interest in her, and it's put her on edge. She's giving the impression that she's the perfect mix of desirable and vulnerable enough to be both valuable and attainable to the likes of Diego. She's brilliant.

The chatter goes on for some time, and I start bracing myself for action; I can hear a stifled mutter from somewhere close to Rosie from time to time, and the age and privilege in the voice makes me suspect it's Morrison. He'll be too insecure next to his own bodyguard's flirting to want him with him when he goes to the bathroom soon.

But then something in Rosie's conversation catches my ear.

"Big bad Italian, huh? No offense, but your friend there doesn't exactly look like he's come right out of Tuscany," Rosie teases, and Diego laughs.

"No, you're right, my client tonight is a proud American. We Italians are branching out more and more these days, you know. The way things are going, I'll likely be working with the Russians like some of my colleagues are, before too long."

My eyes widen, even as I hear the scrape of Morrison's chair over the earpiece. Italians working side by side with Russians? I hadn't heard anything about that, and I was already given some of the details of recent ongoings by my new subordinates in the past few days. The two mafias were usually at odds on the best of days, but for there to be hints of members openly working together…?

If there's collaboration going on under my nose, it could be the missing link that's had Andrei and I vexed over this whole sex slave operation.

But I have no time to reflect further on the development as I watch Morrison come out of the bar and stride down the hall. He makes his way further along, and I put my hand on my pistol as I brace for him to step into the bathroom…

And he passes it by.

My heart catches in my throat. Where would he be going without his bodyguard? Swearing to myself, I stand up and exit the stall, watching him go on my phone. Before I leave the bathroom, I see him go to one of the rooms on the first floor, knocking on the door. Quickly, I exit the bathroom and follow him as though strolling idly down the hallway.

Morrison comes into sight just as the door in front of him opens. As I pass him, I hear him say to the man who opens the door, "Change of plans. Meet me in my room in ten."

The man nods, and the door closes. Morrison now behind me, we're walking in the same direction: to the elevator and stairwell at the end of the hall. With no other choice, I know what I have to do, and I veer off to take the stairs as Morrison enters the elevator.

The moment the elevator doors close, I nearly break into a sprint up the stairs. Morrison is staying on the seventh floor, and I have to beat him there.

If Morrison makes it to his room, the operation is a bust. Andrei should be making the pickup at this very instant, and this cannot look like a smash-and-grab robbery if we're to make it out unscathed. What's worse, I know that if Morrison is heading up the elevator, he'll be contacting his bodyguard to get his flirtatious ass up there with him to make the handoff in his room. This hit has to happen *now*.

My legs carry me faster than I'd have ever hoped, and within a matter of seconds, even as I hear the elevator keeping up with me, I reach the final stairs leading to the seventh floor landing. Glancing up at the cameras on the ceiling, I step into the doorframe of one of the maintenance rooms, into a blind spot, and I take my gun out.

The elevator doors slide open, and I make eye

contact with Morrison for a split second, watching his beady eyes widen before his brains splatter against the wall behind him after I pull the trigger of my gun.

Without missing a beat, I stow the weapon and head back down the stairs, pulling up my text messages to Rosie.

"Done. Car. Now."

The night we arrived back home after the hotel heist, I was too pumped up on adrenaline to sleep, and luckily Konstantin dutifully obliged my enthusiastic chattering. We stayed up until the wee hours of morning, the Bull patiently listening to my ranting re-cap of the night's action while I paced back and forth across the kitchen floor. Even in my state of post-danger high, I couldn't help but pick up on his quiet amusement as he watched me, those gray eyes following my every movement with a twinge of warm fondness. I was still dumbstruck at the fact that we both just participated in an actual jewel heist of cinematic proportions, but Konstantin seemed much more interested in me.

It's strange; as intimidating and dangerous a man as he is, I rarely feel even a hint of fear around him. I am a very intuitive person. I have learned how to read people's moods and body language so well, I'm very nearly psychic at this point. I can sense trouble brewing a mile away, and my instincts have very rarely steered me wrong. I am pragmatic, sensible, and realistic about the world and what it has to offer me — which, in my experience, has not been a whole lot of good. And despite his enormous stature, his gun, his nickname, his vocation, and the dark circumstances under which we met, I find myself oddly at ease with him.

This is especially bizarre when I take into account how very rarely I am ever at ease, period. My life has been one long, serpentine path through hardship after hardship, and after everything I've been through, I don't really ever... relax. I don't allow myself the luxury. Living with the volatile whirlwind of capricious destruction that is my father, I have learned to sleep with one eye open, to constantly look over my shoulder. If not for my own sake, then to better protect Daisy and Sunny.

But with Konstantin, I don't hear that usual alarm bell ringing in the back of my mind. I don't clench my jaw and tense my shoulders. I don't feel like I have to cushion my words and guard my true emotions to the same extent I usually do. I mean, I don't think I will ever be able to fully relax around anyone, or even by myself. The things I have seen and suffered through for the past eight years, especially, have probably scarred me for the rest of my life. However, it does shock me just how quickly I am adjusting to being around the Bull. By all rights, I should fear him. I should despise him. After all, it is partially his fault that I'm stuck here instead of back at home taking care of my sisters. (Though, to be fair, most of the blame is firmly situated on the shoulders of Frank Barnes.)

Of course, the fact that Konstantin has given me space, freedom, and limitless resources to make myself more comfortable in my new environment certainly helps. Even though we have already had sex, he still treats me more or less like a new acquaintance, letting me sleep alone in the huge master bedroom while he sleeps in a room down the hall. Not once has he touched me intentionally, keeping a safe distance between us.

I feel like he might actually respect me, in a way I am not accustomed to.

When we finally go to bed around four in the morning, he stops me just as I am about to walk into my bedroom. There is an almost nervous tinge to his voice when he asks cautiously, "Would you be up for going out tomorrow? To celebrate the success of our mission today, of course."

I blink in confusion for a moment, trying to figure out what exactly he means. It sounds fairly tame, but I still can't help but wonder if there is some ulterior motive. Perhaps he just has another step in the plan, to enact tomorrow. But then the glint in his eyes clues me in — he's asking me… on a date.

"You mean like a date?" I say quietly, hating myself for blushing.

"If you prefer to call it that, yes," the Bull replies coolly. "We met under — less than savory — circumstances, and I would like an opportunity to make it up to you, if you'll have me."

I pause for a moment, waiting for the alarm bell to kick in and start screaming at me to say no, to shut this down before it even has a chance to start. But it never comes. I am left staring up at him with utter silence in my head, for once, as though my instincts have already gone to sleep without me.

Like I've let my guard down for the first time in years.

"Yes, I think I would like that," I hear myself saying, my lips forming the words before my brain can catch up.

"Good," Konstantin agrees, his usually-serious face brightening up as his lips pull back in a wide, genuine smile. I am almost rendered breathless at his incredible handsomeness, the beast having instantaneously transformed into a prince again.

"Wh-where will we go? What are we g-gonna do?" I stammer as he starts to turn away. I'm interested in the answer, of course, but somewhere in my mind it distantly occurs to me that I'm really only asking to keep him here with me a moment longer. I find myself craving another word, another glance from his beautiful gray eyes.

I don't know if I'm just starved for recognition and human contact in general, or if I am genuinely this wrapped up in Konstantin himself.

He looks back at me and shrugs. "I have something in mind, but… it's a secret."

"Oh," I murmur, slightly crestfallen. I do not like surprises. In my experience, they are rarely the good kind. I prefer to know exactly what is coming at any given time, as much as possible. Living with my father is like waking up every morning not knowing whether you're sharing a house with a mildly unpleasant human or a rabid grizzly bear.

"It will be a good surprise, *obeshchayu*," he assures me, the final word leaving his lips in a husky, foreign growl. "I know you will like it."

Konstantin gives me a strangely uncharacteristic wink and heads into his room, leaving me alone and confused in the hallway. I push my door open, still reeling from the sight of a big, scary man like the Bull tossing a roguish wink my way.

I almost want to giggle at his sudden confidence regarding what a girl like me is into, especially because *I* hardly know what I'm into. I haven't exactly gotten many opportunities to explore my more whimsical, fun side. I have only ever been involved with two guys, and I don't think the term "date" could appropriately be applied to the kinds of encounters I had with them.

The first one, a scrawny convenience store cashier three years my senior named Trevor Walsh, used to sneak me free milk and toilet paper in exchange for hurried make-out sessions in the tiny little break room. I was fifteen and he was eighteen, and even at my young age I knew enough about the world to understand how a relatively attractive girl like me could use his crush on me as an advantage. The truth was, I had no money and I needed to find a way to get certain necessities for my household. Making out with Trevor was a marginally less unpleasant plan than simply shoplifting. When he tried to pressure me into having sex right after my sixteenth birthday, I dumped him and got a job at a rival convenience store.

And the second guy was the bassist in a garage band two blocks over. He had a car — an old, beat-up Volkswagen. The guy was considerably more attractive than Trevor, despite the fact that he was also older than me and called himself "The Justinator." His name was Justin Fletcher, and I pretty much only dated him for his car. I was seventeen, it was the fall semester of my senior year of high school, and I needed a way to get around town without having to shell out bus or cab fare. It sounds callous of me, and there were times when I did feel a little guilty about using him, but in my defense, the guy only used me as a pretty prop to make his band mates jealous. Apparently, years ago, Justin's drummer friend stole his girlfriend, and ever since then he'd been trying desperately to regain his stolen sense of manhood. I guess I was a suitable candidate for getting his groove back — until he also started pressuring me to have sex. By then, the school year was ending and summer was on the horizon, reminding me that a work opportunity could present an easier way to afford transportation fare. So, of course, I dumped him immediately.

As I lie in the humongous king-size bed staring up at the ceiling, my mind is racing. I have no idea what to expect from Konstantin. Part of me is still worried that our "date" will just be a rehash of the first night we met — some rushed, humiliating sexual encounter. Or maybe he will actually attempt something vaguely romantic, and it will be awkward, owing to the fact that we are by no means a regular couple. Underneath his compassion toward me is the ugly, underlying truth: he bought me. I am not here of my own free will.

And it's with that dark thought that I fall asleep.

The next morning, I am awakened by the sound of Konstantin knocking lightly at my door. I groan, rub my eyes, and pull the sheets up to my face before muttering, "Come in."

The door creaks open and I peek out from under the blanket to find the Bull dressed in a surprisingly casual ensemble of grey trousers and a black button-down shirt. There's no somber business jacket in sight, and he looks more like a regular — albeit hugely muscled and devastatingly attractive — guy.

I slither out from beneath the covers to walk over to him, dressed only in the oversized T-shirt I've been using as a nightgown for the past few days. I look him up and down a little sheepishly, astonished to find myself so magnetically drawn to him.

"You look… good," I murmur bluntly, my brain not quite awake yet.

He smiles down at me and runs a huge hand back through his dark hair. "Thank you."

"What should I wear?" I ask, tilting my head to one side. I don't know what to expect for today, so I wouldn't know where to even begin, wardrobe-wise.

"Whatever makes you happy. You look beautiful regardless of your attire," Konstantin says simply. "I will leave you to it. Take as long as you need; there's no rush. I will wait for you downstairs."

Once I'm alone, I rush to the en suite master bathroom and hastily jump into the shower, then hurriedly towel-drying my hair and sifting through my drawers to figure out what to wear. I have never once felt nervous about going out with a guy. Granted, the young men I dealt with in the past were scarcely worth getting nervous over, anyway. But Konstantin is a real man — tall and strong, gentlemanly and handsome, regardless of what he does for a living. He did tell me to wear whatever makes me happy. So I take a deep breath, urge myself to relax, and settle on a pair of dark jeans, my black boots, black felt hat, and a white Led Zeppelin shirt made of a soft, fitted material. I look at myself in the elegant floor-length mirror and I'm surprised to find that I look more like myself than I ever have. Like my outside is finally beginning to match my inside, despite the fact that I have been unceremoniously dumped into a totally new environment.

Finally, I head downstairs to meet Konstantin, who rises to smile at me when I walk into the room, gesturing for me to follow him. "You look gorgeous," he says happily, and I can tell he means it. We get into his big black car and he turns on the radio, immediately tuning it to a classic rock station. This kind of music is one of the few things that reminds me of better times, back when my dad used to drive me around town with him when he would run errands, the two of us singing along to Credence Clearwater Revival and Jimi Hendrix.

"Did the shirt clue you in?" I ask, motioning to my Zeppelin shirt.

Konstantin chuckles, a warm, honeyed sound. "Yes, but in my defense, I also have a soft spot for this kind of music. When I was living on the streets of Moscow, my brothers and I would take shelter in a record store. We warmed our frozen bones and listened to the songs. Of course, it was new music to us at the time," he laughs. "Russia has always been a decade or two behind America when it comes to music."

I am taken aback by this sudden glimpse into the Bull's past. "That's kind of sweet," I admit, a smile twitching to my lips. "So, where are we headed?"

"Are you prone to motion sickness?" he asks suddenly, dodging my question. I furrow my brow and give him a dubious look.

"I… I don't think so. Why?"

"Are you afraid of heights?" he continues.

"Maybe a little, I don't know," I reply, squinting at him.

"You'll be okay," he mutters, more to himself than to me.

"Now I'm worried," I admit, biting my lip. Is this some kind of reconnaissance mission? Is he going to tie a rope around my waist and dangle me down through a hole in the ceiling of some high-security vault or something?

"Nothing to worry about, *obeshchayu*," Konstantin says earnestly, glancing over at me.

There's that word again. "What does that mean?" I question.

"It means *I promise*."

"Oh," I say awkwardly. After a moment of tense silence, I burst out, "Please just tell me where we're going, surprises make me nervous. You're not taking me somewhere to kill me, are you?"

Konstantin looks over at me, an expression of pure pity and regret on his face. "Do you really think that's what I want?" he asks quietly.

"No," I answer in a muted voice. I immediately feel terrible for even suggesting it.

"I'm sorry. I should have told you from the start… We're going to Luna Park," he reveals, shrugging. I stare at him with my mouth hanging open for a minute.

"Luna Park? As in, Ferris wheels and funnel cakes?" I clarify dubiously.

I can almost detect the slightest hint of a flush coming over the Bull's sharp, handsome features as he nods. "Yes. I hope that is an acceptable venue for our first date," he says, clearly a little embarrassed. My heart surges with unexpected warmth for him.

"I-I've never been there," I confess. "But I kind of always wanted to."

The smile returns to his face. "Me, too."

KONSTANTIN

The first rays of sunlight of the new day haven't even begin to peak over the water as the battered truck carries me towards the docks. I sit in the passenger's seat, wearing no seatbelt, the old vehicle having lost it for one reason or another long ago, along with one of its side mirrors and the back windshield. The man driving me to our destination has dry, salty skin, and the denim jacket on his shoulders has seen far better days. He has dark skin, and one of his eyes is starting to go cloudy with cataracts, but that doesn't stop him from working every day like any other man who sees himself working the same job for the rest of his life.

He's driving me to a contract I acquired. An assassination that's going to get some attention.

As for me, I'm wearing a dark gray leather jacket over my white tank top, my jeans the same worn pair that I brought with me from Russia. My jacket conceals the star tattooed on my chest, but the man driving me to the docks knows who I am.

He's silent for the drive, but I sense a quiet appreciation for my work. He knows what he's taking me to do.

We finally pull up to the docks, and he leads me through the mess of boats after we clamber out of the old, sputtering truck. He leads me down towards the end of the wooden walkways towards an upscale fishing boat. The name *Fisher King* is written on the side, but it looks like it's used more for revelry than for actual fishing.

The old man moves over to an electrical box on one of the wooden pylons, taking out a key and opening it. He calmly flips one of the switches, and I see the lights — and cameras — around this part of the dock shut off. We have privacy. Nodding to me, the man leads me onto the boat and towards the aft section, where he shows me to the door to the main cabin. He steps aside and turns his gaze to the docks while I step forward and pick the lock, letting it spring open easily.

We step inside so calmly that I think the old man has carried out acts like this before.

Once inside, he takes me to what looks like a wall with a few coats hanging from it. He pushes them aside, flipping a switch the coats concealed and letting the false paneling slide aside smoothly, revealing a small chamber inside, big enough for a couple of people to stand comfortably.

"This is where he keeps them," the old man says, his Russian accent still as thick as the day he stepped onto American shores. "His men have a girl or two hide inside, then he takes the boat out onto the water to fish. The girls come out once they're out on the water, and they have their way with them."

His voice is tinged with the kind of hopelessness experienced only by those who have faced hardship unending their entire lives. I look on the man with a stony expression, but I feel sympathy in my heart. It isn't my place to converse with him, I know. His role in all this is finished. But something in me instills me with a sense of responsibility for this man's well-being. I cannot abide to let him keep suffering.

After all, I lead the immigrants now when everybody else abuses them. I am their leader. I am their guardian. I am their *pakhan*.

"The way you speak of this," I say in Russia, putting a hand on his shoulder as he looks up at me with hardened eyes, "I hear loss in your voice, not fear. You are not a man accustomed to dealing in blood, yet you are confident in this. There is something personal at stake, isn't there?"

The man looks at me a long time before responding slowly. "You hired me to bring you here, *pakhan*. Nothing more. I will say nothing of this to any soul, but I wish you well in whatever you mean to do."

"You know well what I mean to do here," I say, my voice firm. "Tell me, what is this man to you?"

The man's stare is hard, but after a few moments, he turns to the hidden compartment and strokes the wooden walls thoughtfully. "For years," he starts, "I worked these docks. I saw fishermen come and go from all walks of life, from poor men like myself who did this for a living to the rich and wealthy who used these docks to get away from it all. This politician who owns this boat," he says with venom in his voice, referring to the very same man I met on the yacht my first night in Brighton Beach, "Peter Pavlychko, a man nominated for a seat in congress as we speak, he knew me. While I tended his dock from day to day, he watched me raise my family, watched my wife's illness progress and take her from me, watched me raise my only daughter. Watched my daughter grow into a woman."

Tears are in his eyes, and his hands grip the corner of the wall, his knuckles white. "When I had nothing left in life but my daughter, and she had all the world to look forward to, she vanished in the night. An unsolvable case, the police told me, but I know what happened. I know what happens when rich politicians see something they want — the police look the other way, files get lost, evidence gets discredited!"

The old man strides across the room, and I look at his back as he stares out at the sunrise creeping over the edge of the water out the window. "I know he had her taken," he says, his voice choked. "I know he had her taken onto this boat, just like the other girls he brought out here. I was as powerless to save her as I was powerless to save all the other women he had his way with out on the water. I know I'll never see her again." He turns to me, his eyes shining with tears that are too scarce to spill down that dry, cracked face. "I do not know you, *pakhan*, and you do not know me, but you have my cooperation today in exchange for only the knowledge that you will do the justice I could not provide. Avenge my daughter. Please."

I step forward, reaching into my wallet and pulling out several thousand dollars in cash, putting it into the old dock worker's crusted hand. "When I'm done with Brighton," I say, "nobody will face such a fate again. Take this and pay a private investigator to search for your daughter." I watch him close his hand tight around the money and nod silently. "If she's alive, I'll make sure those who would conceal her from sight are dead. Slavers will not be tolerated in Brighton as long as I draw breath."

He looks up at me one last time. "Thank you, *pakhan*," he says in a low tone, and for the first time, I'm glad to have come into leadership in Brighton Beach. The old man leaves, heading back out onto the docks and flipping the power back on before he heads off, back towards his truck.

Without wasting a moment, I step into the compartment and close the door, leaving me in total darkness. In a few hours, I'll be killing a man I shook hands with a few days ago.

The small-time politician who is my target today has more dirt on him than some of the mobsters do. His family came over rich, putting down luxurious roots in New York from the first day. This man is the second in his family to carry on a career in local politics. And that was just what I found out from cursory research.

Deeper digging found even darker secrets. Pavlychko seems to have offered protection to a number of those involved in the international slave trade that Andrei had a hand in shutting down. He escaped Andrei's wave of assassinations by grace of not directly profiting from the trade, but now that there's a power vacuum, he's started to be a consumer again. Ordinarily, he's far too much of a high-priority target for any assassin to take on.

But fortunately for my client, I want to send a message. I want it to be clear that this kind of practice will not be tolerated any longer. Not in my city. So I took it upon myself to complete the contract, and I did not conceal the fact that I am affiliated with the Bratva.

There are more thoughts haunting my mind,

though, even as Andrei and I position ourselves to sweep the city clean of these monsters who trade human flesh. What Diego said back at the hotel still creeps inside my mind, plaguing me with suspicion. Maybe what he said was just a passing remark. In the short time Brighton Beach went without leadership, it's reasonable to think that some of the Russians might have started branching out to the other mafias to get work. They might have even needed to cozy up to them for protection in their time of weakness. Yet when I probed my informants for information about this Italian collaboration, they turned up very little to nothing. Circumstantial evidence, nothing hard. It was supremely frustrating.

But the lack of information is telling in and of itself. If there are Russians working with the Italians, and the Russian slave trade is persisting despite our constant vigilance, then the pieces point toward a troubling implication: there are traitors in the Bratva funneling slave trade through the Italian mafia.

That's a weighty accusation to level, and I have nothing but a few scraps of evidence and no suspects. Anton has dropped off the map, scampered back to Russia for all I know. Or he could be here in Brighton, right under my nose. He knows to keep his distance after the stunt he pulled on the yacht.

So what I do today is as much a challenge to my enemies as it is a job.

Around 8:00 AM, I hear activity outside. A few male voices talking amongst one another, a few laughs here and there. I press myself against the back of the compartment, keeping my body still.

Heavy footsteps get onto the boat — my target Pavlychko, his bodyguards...and someone much smaller, I realize.

I hear the door to the cabin open, and two people enter. A deep, stupid voice says, "You know where to go. Get in there and don't come out until I knock. It'll be about an hour. If I hear so much as a whimper until then, you'll feel it across your face tonight, bitch."

There's no response, but the larger person leaves the room, and I hear a small set of footsteps approach the hidden compartment. A moment later, the door slides open, and I'm faced with a small, dark-skinned woman in swimwear, her eyes widening to the size of dinner plates at the sight of me. Her mouth opens to scream, but I reach out and yank her inside, covering her mouth with one of my large hands as I close the door, sealing us in darkness together.

She's too paralyzed by fear to move for a moment, and I whisper into her ear. "Be calm. You're safe. When he knocks, I will go. You stay."

There's a pause as I feel her trembling under my grip, pressed up against me, but after a few moments, I feel her nod. I wish I could trust her enough to release her, but there's too much at stake for that right now, so I hold her against me, one arm covering her lips while the other arm wraps around her body, pinning her arms to her side as I listen to the activity on the boat.

In time, everyone seems to be on the boat, and I hear the engine start up. I speak once more to the woman in my arms as I hear someone approaching the cabin again. "I promise, you will be safe. But you must be still. Nobody else will touch you today."

Another nod, and I fall silent as the door to the cabin opens, and I hear the guard step inside as the boat starts to move.

The next forty-five minutes pass in noisy silence. The smell of salt grows stronger as we head far out onto the water, feeling the waves roll under us as we stand in that dark room together. Over time, the woman starts to relax, if only a little, and after some time, I feel safe enough to release her. To my relief, she makes no noise, nor hardly moves. She just presses herself against the opposite wall, and I can feel her eyes on me in the darkness, even though we can't see each other.

Voices from outside. It's mostly idle chatter, and I catch a few words about fishing, the weather, and how the weekend has gone. It's remarkable, how callously the rich can carry on their daily lives while paying no regard to the heinous evils they perpetrate on a daily basis. You'd never think the affable man above deck would engage in slavery.

The boat finally comes to a stop, and I imagine we're a fair ways away from the docks, well out into open water. A few minutes later, I hear the sounds of lines being cast as my target begins to fish. There's a tap at the window, and the guard inside the cabin stands up, clearing his throat.

"Alright, cunt," he mutters, "Captain needs a little something to help him relax. It's showtime for you," he says as he slides open the compartment door, and half a second later I stab with precision, blood is running down the hilt of the knife blade I just shoved up under his jaw and into his head, and I hear a stifled gasp from the woman behind me. The burly man's eyes roll up into his head as I withdraw my knife and let him crumple to the ground, dead.

"Wait here," I order her, seeing her in full light for the first time. She can't be a day older than Rosie. I feel my blood boiling under my skin. My target will suffer for what he's been doing.

I close the compartment door once more before stepping towards the exit. Outside, I see two other guards, guns at their side as they patrol the ship. I need to act quickly.

Holding nothing more than a bloody knife, I kick the door to the cabin open right in front of one of the guards, who looks at me, startled. Before he can gain his bearings, I move in and twist his arm behind his back just as the other guard shouts out in alarm, and my target whirls around, dropping his fishing pole in surprise, and his eyes widen at the sight of me.

The second guard is already drawing his pistol, so I turn the first guard in my grip around right before the first few shots go off. The scream of the first guard is silenced when his comrade's own bullets sink into him as I use him as a human shield, and I let him fall to the ground with bullet holes in his head.

Furious, the second guard starts to fire again as I move quickly, but my reflexes are just slow enough for one of the bullets to graze my left arm just as I use my right to hurl the knife at him. I take cover after it leaves my grasp, but the gunshots stop, and I raise my head in time to see the second guard falling to his knees, my knife deep in his throat.

All of this within seconds.

Calmly, I turn my eyes to Pavlychko, who's hardly had time to react. When he realizes what's happened, he starts backing away from me, holding up a hand and shaking his head as I stride towards him, slowly.

"I'd like to see you swim, Peter," I say as he glances at the water, his face white. "But I suspect even the sharks that infest these waters would find your taste too foul."

"Konstantin," he gasps, his hands shaking, "Konstantin listen, you don't have to do this. Wh-what did I do wrong? Okay, I haven't paid my respects, I get it — Sergei was always the type who liked that kind of thing, I just didn't realize you'd be the same, I'm sorry!"

"This is a Bratva matter," I say as I draw closer, "but not that kind. Simpering won't save you today, Peter."

"I-I- I have money!" he splutters, "Girls! Hey, I hear you got a taste of that your first night, and I've got a gal with your name on her in the cabin. Please, just let me go, and the Bratva will never have any trouble in Brighton again, I swear! Name a rival, I'll have the NYPD busting down their doors within *hours*."

"You're getting closer," I say, chuckling as I reach him, grabbing him by the scruff of his collar, "but I'm afraid bribery won't save you. I wonder, do you even know the names of all those women you've burned through over the years?"

His hands are twitchy, and I'm ready for it when he pulls out the knife he was hiding in his pants, catching his wrist easily and squeezing, hearing it break under my grasp, and I toss him to the back of the boat as he howls in pain over his broken wrist.

"You don't know what you're doing," he hisses at last, glaring daggers at me. "You'll have the whole fucking city hounding you for killing me. Do you even know who I am?"

While he's been speaking, though, I've picked up the spare anchor on deck, holding the weighted metal in one hand while coiling up the rope in the other as I approach Pavlychko, kicking him in the side as I reach him.

"A dead man," I say candidly while I wrap the rope around his legs and tie it.

As he realizes what I'm doing, he starts stammering incoherently for a moment before he gets his bearings to splutter out, "Anton! You want Anton, don't you?"

I raise my eyebrow at him in question. He's right, but I don't want to look too interested, or he might start making demands.

"I-I don't know where he is, I swear! He's been off the radar ever since he started working with the Italians!"

There it is.

I smile at Pavlychko as I pick him up and take him to the back of the boat, turning the engine on, blades spinning under the water as the boat moves. "I know, Peter," I say in a low growl to him. "And don't worry. He'll answer for twice again as much as you have."

Pavlychko lets out a nervous laugh, nodding. "Right! So, you let me go, I help you go after the Italians, and we forget this ever happened, right?"

I glare at him with a stony gaze. "You rich people. You always expect that your crimes can go away with a gesture, a wave of your cash, that you can buy innocent lives and pay your way out of the consequences."

Pavlychko gasps as I lift him up, and I hurl him screaming into the water near the engine, and blood darkens the water around the boat as the blades slice him to pieces while the anchor carries his remains deep down to the ocean floor, the dark figure of his body vanishing from sight after a few seconds as I stare after him.

"Not in my city."

It's been a few days since Konstantin took me to Luna Park on our first real date, and every day has been full of surprises. I can't believe how bizarrely like a real relationship this feels, like we're a normal boyfriend and girlfriend who just happened to meet under unfortunate circumstances. It's not like we spend every moment together, which is kind of a relief, since I am still getting used to living with him in the first place. Besides, I don't think I will ever really be the kind of girl who wants to spend every waking second glued to my partner's side, even under the best conditions. Konstantin gives me my space, allowing me the freedom to feel independent even though I am essentially still his captive.

It's getting difficult to think of him as my captor, though, especially when I think about how sweet and relaxed our day at Luna Park was. The two of us walked around the brightly-colored amusement park, breathing in the sugary-salty air and taking in the whirring machinery and laughter mingled with exhilarated screams. I had never been to an amusement park in my life, and my only knowledge of them came from years of watching television. I was totally overwhelmed with everything going on around us. Luna Park was like every color, smell, and sound all dumped into an ear-splitting blender of chaos. It was strange how I felt more nervous on a date with Konstantin than I'd felt during our high-risk jewel heist.

But luckily my date remained cool and collected, taking me on the milder rides like the spinning teacups and the seaside swings before we moved on to the roller coasters and thrill rides. I never expected I would be afraid of something a child would ride on, but since this was a totally new world for me, I was oddly anxious. As we strapped ourselves into the decades-old, rickety Cyclone, my heart rate picked up and I found myself instinctively reaching out to take Konstantin's hand across the seat. His fingers found mine, sending a shiver of warm comfort, just as the ride jolted us forward to begin.

After that, we laughed at each other's exhilarated ruddy cheeks and tousled hair, then walked hand-in-hand to get drinks and a funnel cake to share. It was a testament to Konstantin's suave persona that he somehow managed not to get a single smear of bright white sugar on his black shirt. I, however, ended up with powdered sugar in my hair and down my jeans. But the Bull only gently laughed and shrugged it off, telling me it was "all just part of the experience." I am continually impressed by just how down-to-earth he seems to be, underneath that big, bad mafia mask. It's almost like he's a real person with real feelings and thoughts instead of a brutish robot trained to obey.

And I am finding myself powerfully, unintentionally growing fond of him.

Konstantin possesses the unique superpower of making me forget my usual stressors. He is so kind, so intent on listening to me and making me feel comfortable, that he manages to steal my full attention. It's difficult to think about being anywhere else, doing anything else, when he's with me. I don't think I have ever been so single-minded in anything besides my all-consuming responsibility to take care of Sunny and Daisy.

Of course, whenever Konstantin leaves me to my own devices, I spend nearly the entire time obsessing over how I will get back to them, worrying incessantly about whether they have food to eat, if they're remembering to take their baths and brush their teeth. So many times I have almost brought them up to Konstantin, their names balancing just on the tip of my tongue. But something always stops me. Almost as though I am terrified to shatter the near-fantasy that my life has turned into since coming to live with the Bull.

And then, of course, I am wracked with heart-shattering guilt for thinking that.

I can't help but feel terribly selfish for enjoying my time here, not knowing whether my sisters are okay or not. More than once, after Konstantin has retired to his bedroom and I am sitting alone in my own giant bed, I have pulled the computer onto my lap and searched for my house on Google Street View. I know the images haven't been updated in years, but I still sit there and stare at the peeling white siding of our tiny, shotgun-style home on the computer screen as though I might be able to teleport there just by staring at it hard enough.

It's not like I'm exactly homesick; my house has never been a safe place for me or my sisters. A house is just a house, unless the memories you've made there are powerful and bright enough to generate their own kind of spirit. Our trailer in Mississippi was imbued with my mother's shining soul, present still in faint traces even after she died. But the Jersey house is nothing but an empty shell, a crash pad for an alcoholic deadbeat and his three daughters who live in fear of his every homecoming.

I wish there was a way to check in on the girls. If only I could ask Konstantin to let me visit home or even just call the house. But I don't have my own phone here, and part of me is still afraid to trust Konstantin with my address and the knowledge that I have two tiny, vulnerable little sisters there. I want so badly to trust him. He has certainly done everything in his power to convince me he can be trusted.

But the thought of the sadistic fuckers who sold me like a hunk of prized meat finding out about Daisy and Sunny chills me to the very bone. I can only hope that my dad hasn't told anyone about them. Last night I had a nightmare that the lead mafia guy from the yacht broke into my house and kidnapped the girls. I woke up hyperventilating, tears sticky on my cheeks.

I think Konstantin caught onto my anxious mood, because he has arranged a kind of platonic date for me — with the young wife of his business partner, Andrei. I am a little nervous about meeting her, as I have not had a lot of close friends in my lifetime. I mostly played by myself growing up, and once the girls were born, I essentially aged several years in an instant, making me a strange companion for other carefree kids my age. It's hard to maintain a friendship when every waking moment of your life revolves around taking care of two small children. A bit difficult for other pre-teens to relate to.

So today, Konstantin gave me a wad of cash and dropped me off at an outdoor shopping outlet, stating that my play date would arrive any minute.

He handed me a disposable cell phone just before he drove off, giving me a wide, reassuring smile as he rolled up the window. I know there's no reason to feel nervous, really — I am fiercely independent and if there's one thing I should be able to handle, it's a girls' day out.

Even if my date is probably the hardened, tough-talking wife of a hitman.

Of course, I am totally surprised when the young woman who approaches me with a big smile on her face is actually a petite, dainty-looking blonde in a white sundress and floppy hat, a grinning baby boy on her hip. She waves at me and then sticks out a tiny white hand for me to shake. I can't help but feel like a tall, black rain cloud next to this luminescent ball of sunshine.

"Hi, my name is Cassie, and I'm assuming you are Rosalie?" she asks, her voice just as sweet and soft as her appearance. The little boy giggles and reaches out for me instantly. "Oh, I think Max likes you!" Cassie laughs.

"You can call me Rosie," I tell her, letting the toddler wrap his pudgy hand around my pointer finger. "Forgive me for saying this, but you are so not what I expected," I admit.

Cassie shrugs and gestures for me to follow her. "Oh, I'm used to that. No offense taken. I gave up a long time ago on trying to be what other people expect me to be. Nowadays I'm just myself, and that seems to work out just fine," she explains candidly. I am immediately drawn to her. She is so upbeat and gentle, she reminds me of my mother. Max lets out a little whimper and reaches for me again as we start strolling down the promenade. Cassie offers him to me and I instinctively accept, used to carrying babies.

"Huh, you're a natural!" she exclaims. "You've got to have a little one at home, right?"

"Well, actually…" I begin, trailing off. Perhaps two seconds into my first encounter with this woman is not the best time to jump headfirst into a narrative of my complicated, fucked-up life. But she only looks at me expectantly, and I get the sense that maybe there is something dark in her past, too. Like she might just understand what I come from.

So at her gentle prodding, I dive into an explanation of my home life, how I've had to raise my little sisters pretty much all on my own, how I have struggled to survive for eight years. She listens intently and patiently, seeming to fully engage with even the darkest details I reveal. Not even once do I feel like she's judging me negatively; in fact, her responses are so supportive and understanding that for the first time I feel a little less alone in the world, less ashamed of who I am and what I come from.

"My goodness," Cassie says, shaking her head as we walk into a little boutique. "You have been through so much. You must be a very strong person.

Actually, we have a lot in common, you and I. My father… he sold me, too. That kind of betrayal is difficult to put aside, I will admit. Your pain is still fresh, I can tell. But I can assure you that it will get better. Those old wounds don't hurt me like they used to. Especially with a man like Andrei by my side."

There's a strength in her voice when she says her husband's name that tells me their love is pure and powerful. "Your husband… you met him the same way Konstantin found me?"

Cassie nods, perusing a shelf of gauzy pale pink blouses I would never wear, but would look amazing on her. "Much the same, yes. And at first, I was terribly embarrassed. Hurt. But now I can say with confidence that it was the best thing to ever happen to me. The only problem was how much I missed my little brother. I know you can relate to that."

I feel a twinge of heartache, my sisters' faces popping into my mind's eye.

Cassie reaches out and places a soft hand on my shoulder. "Just tell Konstantin what you're feeling. I don't know him very well, but I can tell you that a friend of Andrei's is a good man. You can trust him. These men in the Bratva — many of them come from terribly dark places, lonely and cold. Their brothers in arms are the only family they know. Forgive them their trespasses, if you can manage. Sometimes when I used to look back in horror on the things my Andrei did years and years ago, I reminded myself that you do things for family you would never do otherwise."

"That is definitely true," I agree, thinking back to the times I used my body, my sex appeal, just to get necessities for my family. I used those filthy guys, and they used me. But if I were dumped into the same situation, I would do it all again in a heartbeat.

Cassie and I spend the rest of the sunny afternoon going through the shops, sharing stories about our childhoods, bonding over how bizarre our lives have been. Considering Cassie just on face value, I never would have expected the two of us to have anything in common. Looks-wise, we are about as opposite as two girls can be. Her style is frilly and floaty, while mine is a lot closer to punk rock or grunge. But we get along wonderfully, and by the time late afternoon is rolling around, I am sad to see her go. But Max is getting cranky, and it's time for him to go home and take a nap.

"This was so much fun," Cassie says earnestly, and I agree with her. I never knew how cathartic it could be to confide in someone who truly seems to understand. "Are you sure you don't want me to drive you back home? It really wouldn't be any trouble at all," she offers.

"No, no. It's fine. I actually kind of miss getting to take public transportation, believe it or not," I tell her with a laugh. And it's true; after years of being so independent and self-reliant, it feels strange to have anyone cart me around like a small child. I can find my own way home.

"Well, then, I won't take that away from you," she says with a wink. "Hope to see you soon! And I know Max will be dying to see you again, too. He seems to really like you."

The angelic, chubby-cheeked toddler is nodding off in his bright red car seat, a toy truck clutched on his lap. I feel a surge of vaguely maternal fondness wash over me. It may just be due to how long I spent being a surrogate parent to my sisters, but I do really love children. Their innocence and complete lack of guile is refreshing in comparison to the darkness I know lurks around every corner.

"Yeah, you'll definitely see me again," I assure her, smiling. We say our goodbyes and I hail a cab, spending the whole drive home thinking about how much better I feel now. I can't help but wonder if Konstantin did this on purpose to make me feel less afraid of him or something. Either way, I feel indebted to him for giving me this breath of fresh air. He trusts me enough to hand me a thick stack of hundred-dollar bills and set me loose on the city. For all he knows, I could be halfway back to Jersey by now.

But something is pulling me back home… to my new home. My eclectic, over-the-top castle in the sky with my sweet, powerful beast of a housemate.

When I arrive home, I see that his car is in the driveway. I walk into the house and up the stairs, heading for my bedroom. Then, I stop suddenly in the hallway, looking over at the door to Konstantin's chambers. Something in my stomach twists, my heart skipping a beat. Almost as though in a trance, I walk over and open the door to find him seated at a massive, glossy mahogany desk, bent over a stack of papers and maps. He looks over in surprise.

"I didn't expect you home so soon," he says, and I hear the true meaning in his words: *I didn't expect you to come home at all.*

"I guess I just missed you or something," I answer, shrugging. But it's more than that.

I want to be here.

I want to be with him, whatever that means.

He stands up just as I walk over to him, his full imposing height towering over me. There is a tense pause as we simply size each other up, searching each other's eyes for answers to questions neither of us dare to ask.

And before any words can arise to spoil the moment, we lean into each other, our lips meeting in a passionate kiss. His arms wrap around me and pull me close, his fingers wrapping in my hair, tossing my black hat down onto the desk as he walks me backward to the bed. With one effortless motion, he scoops me up and cradles me back onto the bed, kissing a delicate line down my jaw, nipping lightly at my neck at first, then sucking harder to leave rosy little marks.

Feeling both terrified and electrified, I peel off my clothes with shaking hands while he wordlessly does the same. When he stands before me, utterly naked and rippling with powerful musculature, I almost want to recoil in fear. This is a man who could easily snap me in half.

But the softness, the pure adoration and wonder in his eyes, assures me he never would.

Konstantin leans down over me and brushes the hair back from my face, his thumb tracing loving circles on the apple of my cheek. He kisses me deeply, his other hand trailing down to stroke my clit. I whimper into his mouth and roll my hips involuntarily, spurring him to lift me up and place me on his lap as he sits back against the pillows. His hard, massive length rubs tantalizingly against my wet slit, making me want him even more. His hands caress my breasts, my hips, my ass, while his lips kiss and suck the tender flesh of my neck. Shivers of pleasure travel down my spine, and before long I can't wait anymore.

"I need you… now," I murmur. "But I don't know what I'm doing."

"I will guide you," he says softly, his thumb tracing across my full lower lip.

He reaches down and lifts me up slightly, positioning the head of his shaft at my slick opening. He nods, signaling me to lower myself onto him.

With one smooth, mind-blowing movement, I let him spear me, my legs straddling him. Suddenly, every ounce of self-consciousness dissipates, leaving only a single-minded desire to feel closer to Konstantin, to feel him fill me up entirely.

We quickly find a steady rhythm, his hands holding me in place as I ride him. Even though I'm in control, it feels more like a shared effort, like we have one shared mind, one mutual mission to reach that most glorious pinnacle of bliss. His lips fall open as I bounce up and down, swiveling my hips forward and backward, feeling him strike that place deep inside that makes me see stars, again and again, until we're both crying out. I grab hold of his shoulders in desperation, trying to brace myself, and he places his hands on my hips, holding me still while he thrusts up into me. I am distantly amazed at his overpowering strength and stamina.

His rhythm becomes more and more erratic and frantic, until finally a wave of intense pleasure seizes my whole body. I collapse onto his chest just as he thrusts upward one more time, filling my cunt with his hot, thick honey. We lie together, panting, breathing in each other's scent, for hours, without speaking — almost as though we're both petrified that uttering a single word might shatter the damn near magical stillness of our tiny world.

"Relax your shoulders."

"They're relaxed."

"Loosen them more, you should feel the weight of your arms."

"Okay."

"How does it feel in your hand?"

"Heavy."

"Good. Use its weight, feel comfortable wielding it."

"I've got it."

"Shoulders relaxed. *Now.*"

In a flash, Rosie whirls around on her heels and hurls the knife in her hand at the target I've set up in the back of the manor, the blade sailing towards the cutout of a man just as I'd taught her to throw it. Her eyes are on the target, but before she can see whether it strikes true or not, I decide to put more of her training to the test.

My hand wraps around her wrist, jerking her back towards me, and to my delight, I feel her twist out of my grip as fluidly as though she were made of pure water, slipping away and facing me before her knee flies up to my side to strike me, and my arm comes down to parry it out of the way effortlessly, but another blow comes in from her fist to my torso.

We trade blows and blocks as we begin to spar, and I can see the training of the past couple of weeks really coming out in her. Despite how she tenses when my eyes are on her, when it comes down to the action, she keeps her body loose and quick, and when she comes in with a blow, her laterals are tight while her shoulder relaxes, and I can feel real force behind the strike when she manages to land one.

She uses our height difference to her advantage. I'm fast, and it's not truly fair for training purposes that I can keep up with her so easily, but then again, a real fight will never be fair, so I see it as an added boon that she has me to train with. Her legwork is impeccable, and if I weren't so ready to anticipate the very moves I'd taught her, she'd have me tumbling to the ground in a matter of moments.

I come in with a strike to her gut, but she whirls around it, using my own arm as a point of stability to push herself around me, and to my genuine surprise, I feel a weight lift from my side as she grabs my own knife from its sheath, drawing it out and putting the blade to my back, forcing me to put my hands up, and the commotion settles, leaving us with the sound of our breathing in the morning air as a smile spreads across my face.

"You learn quickly," I say, glancing back at her. The next moment, my leg sweeps behind me, and she yelps as she starts to fall to the ground. I catch her fall with one arm under her back while wrenching the knife loose from her grip with the other, putting the knife to her, and it's her turn to turn her head up, smirking at me.

"Alright, point taken," she says, and I help her to her feet, putting my knife away and dusting myself off.

"When you pin someone with a knife like that, it helps to keep the weapon in view," I explain. "An enemy is less willing to take risks like that when the threat is visible."

"You just knew I wouldn't really stick a knife in your back," she retorts, crossing her arms with a playful smile.

"Do you think that changes anything?" I reply, arching an eyebrow, but before she can respond, I nod my head towards the target she'd thrown the knife at earlier.

The hilt sticks out of the target's neck, bobbing in the wind. Rosie smiles, and the smile splits into a grin before she can help it.

The shooting range I've set up for her has been going in similar fashion. The first few days, my pistol sat uncomfortably in her hand.

"I don't like the way this thing feels," she'd said, testing the gun's weight.

"You shouldn't," I'd said. "They're wicked devices. But you must learn to use one, if you mean to defend yourself in every way possible."

And she proved to me that she was capable of doing just that. She's a natural shooter, and the precise clusters of bullet holes in the targets I set up for her are testaments to that.

"You know," I say as I walk with her to the target to retrieve her knife, "I don't think I taught you how to use my own blade against me like that. You're getting creative. This is good."

"I thought it might be a little dangerous to test those reflexes of yours," she admits, and I can almost see the playful smile on her face behind me, "but I figured it would be worth the risk to see how you'd counter it. Gotta be ready for those things in real life, isn't that what you keep saying?"

A small smile forms on my face as I take the hilt of the knife and yank it out of the dummy, tossing it up into the air and catching it by the blade as it falls, flipping it over as she steps closer to me, eyeing the knife. Instinctively, I wrap a hand around her waist and draw her closer, surprising her, but she wraps her hands around my torso as well, her hands exploring my muscles as I feel her desire starting to awaken.

"You've learned so much, very quickly," I say in a low tone, looking down at her, and she bites her lip a moment before speaking.

"I've got quite a teacher," she says.

"There's still so much I want to show you," I reply, my hand sliding around to her ass, and she gasps as I give it a squeeze. "But I need to know that you trust me."

"I trust you enough to grab a knife from your side," she teases, and for the first time in a long time, my teeth flash in a grin.

I descend upon her, my lips pressing into hers, and her eyes close as I pick her up and carry her back inside. Her hands begin moving about my sides and my back so voraciously, her hips pressing up needfully, that I hardly think we'll make it to the bedroom. So once we're inside the manor, past the kitchen, and into the main hallway, I sit her down on one of the large, spacious couches, letting her limbs sprawl out on it as her eyes flutter open to look up at me.

The desire in them fans the fire within me as I strip my shirt off slowly, and her eyes rove up and down my body, taking in everything that I am.

"Get a good look, *zvyozdochka*," I say in a low tone, reaching into my pocket, my fingers brushing against the silk fabric I'd had stored away there before I pull out the long, black cloth that she eyes, her cheeks reddening a bit. "For now, you're going to be relying on your other senses."

She nods cautiously, and she does not resist as I step around her and bring the blindfold over her eyes, tying it gently behind that soft black hair of hers, and I let my hands slide down her neck, then down to the edge of her shirt, which she lets me pull up over her head, exposing her sports bra, and I remove that as well, leaving her chest bare before me, lying on the couch like prey.

I put a knee on the couch, looming over her as she turns her head, her chest rising and falling as she breathes, cheeks flushing with color as she feels me near.

"Did you enjoy grabbing my knife, Rosie?" I whisper into her ear as my hand goes to my side, and I let the blade audibly scrape against the holster as I draw my knife, and she takes in a breath sharply before she gives a slight nod. One of my hands takes her smaller one, then the other hand, and I push them to the arm of the couch over her head, holding her chest and stomach exposed before me.

Bringing the blade to her bare skin, I let the cool metal touch her stomach, and she gasps, her hands clenching. "Don't move," I whisper as I start to trace the dagger up to her breasts and around her chest. "Do you trust me, Rosie?"

"With my life," she breathes, and there's no fear in

her voice that doesn't thrill her in my grasp, her hips squirming even as she does her best to keep her torso still.

"Good," I say as I bring the knife up to her neck, the point of the blade upside-down as I let it play across the sensitive skin, her usually pale face flushed bright red. "You've come so far, but if I am to train you, we need to be able to rely on each other entirely." I bring the blade lower on her body, tracing around her side and getting closer to the opening of her pants, and with a flick of my fingers, I open the front of her jeans and wiggle them down off of her. She doesn't wear anything under them, and her warm lips sit exposed before me. Slowly, I bring the knife around her pelvis, drawing the tip close to that most sensitive spot, but never touching it.

As the knife plays across her inner thigh, she manages to speak through the quickening breaths. "And do you trust me, Konstantin? Can you rely on me?"

I pause in my knife's path, then pick the blade up and slowly place it in her hand, guiding her hand to hold the thing against my bare chest as I smile down on her blindfolded face. Slowly, so slowly, she guides the dagger around my muscles, moving as expertly as I did without a blindfold, and so gently I can hardly feel a thing on me, save for the ripple of electricity I feel when it grazes near my nipple. "More than I thought I'd ever trust another human, Rosie."

After that, she lets the knife drop to the side of the couch, and I descend upon her again, pressing my lips into hers as I grind my stiff cock against her. The moment she feels my hardness, she starts pressing herself up to me in desire.

My mouth goes to her chest, and she lets out a yelp as my teeth graze her stiffening nipples, their hardness obeying my motions as I use my tongue to awaken them. Her shoulders and head roll back as I ravish her, my hands greedily holding onto her hips as I attack her nipples. My cock is threatening to burst from my pants as I grind against her, her thigh pressing up against it. I feel her rubbing it, daring me to go farther, to push her harder, and I grin even as my teeth brush up and down her nipples.

She wants me, and she wants to see what I can do, in the field and in bed. I've never seen such spirit in a woman before.

I move my hands down to free my cock from its restraints, but as she hears me doing so, I notice her hands groping for mine, trying to push them aside so she can do the deed herself. I raise my eyebrows as she undoes my pants and lets my shaft spring forth, and at her warm touch, my crown bulges dark and hard for her. The deep, satisfied sigh I hear as she grasps my cock, enjoying the feel and weight of it in her hands, is indescribably satisfying.

She gives my hip a slight tug as if begging me to move forward, and I oblige, sliding my shaft up to her blindfolded face, her mouth opening in desire. It takes no time for her to guide herself to my crown, pressing her lips to it experimentally. At the touch of her warm, soft lips, my dark crown throbs, a low, soft moan escaping my lips, and that spurs Rosie on to open her mouth wider and take the whole crown into her mouth.

The warmth of her tongue washing over my cock sends a wave of energy through me, and I feel like my lower muscles are uncoiling. I feel like we were made for each other as her mouth slides over my cock so effortlessly, her light moaning lulling me into a near trance as one of her hands feels my balls, reveling in the sensation of having me within her. The more she finds she can fit into her mouth, the more her enthusiasm builds, and she sucks at my cock with hunger as her tongue lashes around it fiercely.

She tastes my precum as it beads out the tip of me, devouring it as if we'd been doing this for years, and I can sense her own pride in herself as she makes my knees feel weak beneath me, and I have to lean harder on the couch, my whole mass looming over her.

Finally, I gently withdraw my cock as I feel my balls start to tighten. "Not yet, *zvyozdochka*," I whisper in a low husk as her mouth lingers open, glistening with desire for me. "You should be rewarded for your hard work, first."

Before she can respond, I slide my fingers to her clit, rubbing two fingers around it in a circle, and she starts to clench her thighs together on reflex, but I keep them apart, leaving her to squirm in vain and whimper as I torture her with my fingers, her fingers clenching into the couch. She's already pent up, the energy of our training together spurring her on in her desire for me, and mine for her, and I can feel her start to tense under me...and again, I deny her, withdrawing my fingers just before I push her over the point of no return.

"Fuck you," she gasps, her mouth curled up in a smile as she brings her cheek to her shoulder as she moves around under me, and I let out a chuckle, bringing my mouth to her neck. I have to restrain myself from biting her there as my hand moves under the small of her back, and as I pepper the sensitive nape of her neck with kisses, I press my cock's crown to her lower lips, leaving it there teasingly, holding her hips down as she tries to press up into me.

"Please," she whimpers at last, "I want you to fill me up completely, Konstantin."

When we intertwine our bodies, and her lips hug the base of my cock and fill me with warmth as I send sensation pulsing through her body, we both can't hold back our moans as I start to buck into her.

Despite our knifeplay, there's nothing violent in how we press into each other, and the aggression we feel meshes together so vividly that I can't tell where the fire burning within me for her ends and her own warmth begins. She gives me a warmth I've never felt before, utterly overwhelming and filling, even as I feel myself start to grow tense to fill her.

We're so keyed up that we waste no time in growing more desirous in our motions, and she clenches her cunt around me, knowing full well what she's spurring me on to as I buck into her hard and fast, feeling my bulging crown stroke her inner walls as her mouth starts to hang open. My hips move faster and faster, and finally, she throws her head back and lets out a scream that fills the entry hallway as I release myself within her, feeling every shot of hot seed that spills into her body, pouring all of myself into Rosie as she continues to clench herself around me, alternating between utter relaxation and passionate desire to take all that I want to offer her.

My cock is still stiff inside her when we descend from our shared climax, and finally, I brush the blindfold away from her eyes, which flutter open to see me and my glistening chest looming over her. I smile, and she gives a playful laugh back that's cut short as I pull out of her, some of our intermingled fluids spilling out as I do, and I use a cloth sitting on a nearby table to help clean her up.

"Enough training for one day?" she breathes, smiling.

"Maybe enough for a break," I concede, giving her a pat on the ass as she stands up to gather her clothes and put them back on. I start to head upstairs once we're fully dressed, but she catches me around the waist, playfully pulling me back toward the couch, and I can't help myself but laugh as I let myself fall onto it with her, scooping her up in my arms and kissing her cheeks while we still glow from our activities.

"There's still much information to gather," I say a few minutes of embracing later, pressing my forehead to hers, but Rosie wears a frown on her face. I know she worries about me when I go out on these little reconnaissance expeditions to gather intel, but if we're to maximize our success, I need to be able to move quickly and quietly on my own. Plus, setting up my own band of loyal followers requires me to be present with them.

"I don't doubt you can take care of yourself," she says, "I...just worry, is all. About a lot of things. Don't get me wrong," she adds quickly, "you've done more than I could possibly imagine to keep as many people safe as you can, but...maybe I've just been trained after all this time to think about the worst."

I frown as I stroke her cheek with a furrowed brow. "Never feel like you need to hide such concerns from me, Rosie. What's on your mind? If it makes you feel better, I'm going to have some guards around the house soon — men I know I can trust, who Andrei and I have vetted thoroughly."

"It's not me I'm worried about," she says, glancing up at me. "It's my sisters."

I nod slowly. She's mentioned her sisters before, but I think they're such a sensitive subject for her that she's slow to bring it up. "I can arrange to have them brought here, if you wish. Only say the word."

"No," she says quickly, "with everything that's going on, with all the people who might be targeting us soon, I think they're safest where they are now. But do you think there's any way we could...I don't know, keep any eye on them somehow? I know that must sound stupid to you, but-"

"I understand entirely, Rosie," I say firmly, taking her hand in mine and pausing a moment before continuing. "When I was a boy in Moscow, I had nobody to raise me. There are many such kids like that in the city, and the Russian winters grow bitterly cold. I was always a tall boy, even back then, and over time, many of the young ones came to...sort of look up to me, like an older brother."

I play with her fingers in my hand while she stares at my face while I tell her the story, something I haven't spoken much about since, well, since it was happening.

"We looked out for each other. We stole for each other, we taught each other, we fought for each other, and when the times became too hard for some of us to bear," I hesitate, "we mourned for each other." I look her in the eye and squeeze her hand. "Rosie, I can't imagine what you've had to do for your sisters in the house you grew up in. I know they must be the closest people in the world to you. I'll have someone check in on them daily for you. Not a thing will happen in that house that we don't hear about."

Rosie squeezes me back, and a faint smile appears on her face before she nods. "Thank you, Konstantin. And hey," she adds as I rise to my feet. "Be careful out there."

I flash a smile back at her as I head to get the rest of my gear. "For you? Maybe I will."

I never knew how wonderful it can feel to wake up next to someone. For the past month or so, we have been sleeping together every night in the bedroom originally designated as mine. The time we've spent together has been a whirlwind of subtle changes, the two of us spinning closer and closer together with every passing day. I feel like this has to be some kind of strange fever dream, like I'm going to wake up any moment now on the uncomfortable futon back at my father's house.

Of course, I do still miss my sisters. Desperately. The pangs of intense guilt are still a fairly common occurrence for me, as my mind travels ever back again to Daisy and Sunny, worrying about whether they're okay. But luckily, Konstantin has been incredibly understanding in regards to my situation, enlisting the service of an extremely professional and discreet private investigator to check in on them daily. The man's name is Ilya Kovak, and he is about as somber as a corpse, but he gets the job done.

He managed to break into my old house — which really isn't that impressive a feat considering the fact that my dad forgets to lock the doors most of the time — and quickly install a surveillance system. So even when Ilya isn't physically nearby to keep an eye on the girls, his live camera feed is constantly rolling. To my dismay, both he and Konstantin argued against allowing me access to the feed, assuming (correctly) that I would become totally consumed with watching it. Ilya promises to keep a close eye on the situation back home, and to alert me at the first sign of the kind of danger requiring action on our part.

Just as I suspected, my dad is more or less ignoring the girls, leaving them to fend for them-selves. But I did such a thorough job of training the twins that they are fairly self-sufficient, actually, even though they are only children themselves. I try to remind myself that I was scarcely older than they are when I was forced to take on the full-time oblig-ation of caring for two infants. So, if I could handle that on my own, then surely the two of them can survive.

And to my infinite relief, they do spend most of their time either at the public library or at Ms. Liddell's house. They recently turned nine years old, and my heart aches to think that I wasn't there for their birthday. But Ilya assures me that they had a relatively good day; Ms. Liddell and the girls ordered pizza and baked cupcakes, then spent the evening playing board games and watching old black-and-white movies. When I asked Ilya how he had such a vivid picture of what happened that day despite not having any surveillance equipment in Ms. Liddell's house, he simply said, "I watch. Nobody sees me. I am very good at my job."

And that was that. I do worry that the girls think I have intentionally abandoned them, or that I've died or something. That is what hurts the most — not being able to tell them I'm okay, that I'm *more* than okay, I'm actually the closest to happy I've been in a long, long time. Except for the fact that there's a void in my heart where the girls used to be. But I can't tell them anything about what's going on, because that might catapult them into danger. The business of taking down segments of the mafia is a treacherous one, and I have already accepted that my life may never be safe. But I refuse to allow this often dark, cruel world intersect with the lives of Daisy and Sunny. Even if that means I will never get to see them again, or even speak to them.

I turn over in bed, sighing. I reach out instinctively for Konstantin, only to find the spot beside me empty. I sit up in bed and look around, then notice the faint patter of water falling. He's in the shower. A smile hitches itself to my lips as I slide out of bed and pad across the room into the en suite, hot steam enrobing me with warmth.

Through the faint fog I can see the Bull's massive, muscular frame outlined behind the silvery-white shower curtain. This is one of my favorite places to find him — naked, wet, and hot.

I try to walk quietly over, but just as I'm reaching to pull back the curtain, Konstantin's baritone voice murmurs, "I know you're there, *ptichka*."

"How do you do that?" I sigh, bemused and frustrated. "I was *so* quiet!"

"Call it a sixth sense," he laughs, peering around the curtain at me with shampoo foaming up on top of his head. He somehow manages to still look handsome.

"May I come in?" I ask demurely. He nods and disappears behind the curtain again, leaving me to hastily strip out of my panties and oversized T-shirt. Gingerly, I slip in behind him.

Immediately my body relaxes at the welcoming embrace of hot water. Until I came to live here, I never understood the true meaning of a long, hot shower. Growing up, my dad often forgot to pay the water bill, causing us to sometimes go several days without water. And even when the bills were on time, we always lived in such rundown places that water pressure and heat were… spotty at best. I took a lot of very brief, weak, cool showers.

Of course, the best part of taking a shower here had more to do with the hot body pressed up against me than the hot water itself.

Konstantin washes the shampoo out of his hair and gives me more space to stand directly under the stream. I tug my hair down from its loose bun, shaking it out and letting the water pulse down my scalp. I take a deep, contented breath, just as Konstantin wraps his thick arms around me and presses a soft kiss to my forehead.

"You're up early," he says. "I hope I didn't wake you."

"I wouldn't miss this for the world," I murmur, sliding my palms down his powerful, slick chest. He bends slightly to kiss me hard on the lips, his own hands gripping my ass, pulling me close to him. I can feel his cock stirring to life, stiffening against my belly. I break free of his embrace and instantly sink to my knees, wrapping my fingers around his massive length. I glance up to see his gray eyes roll back and shut, his hands tangling in my hair to gently guide me.

I tease him at first, just flicking my tongue around the crown of his shaft, moving my hands loosely up and down his length. I love feeling him grow harder under my touch. It makes me feel powerful, sexy in a way I never knew I could be.

Then I slowly, tantalizingly take him into my mouth, my tongue pushing up against the underside of his cock. Konstantin groans and gently pushes forward so that the tip brushes against the back of my throat. I am surprised at how naturally this comes to me, since I had virtually no sexual experience before meeting the Bull. But something about him, the way we just fold into each other like we were made to fit... I'm finding out more about myself than ever.

Starting to bob back and forth on his cock, I grip the backs of his thighs to steady myself, sucking harder and harder until he's nearly fucking my mouth, his hips rolling with every stroke. I can feel that he's getting close, his fingers tightening in my hair, his groans growing louder and less inhibited. But before he comes, he suddenly pushes me back gently. I let out an involuntary whimper of disappointment, not wanting to stop. Instead, Konstantin gestures for me to stand up.

He cups my breasts, deftly sliding his thumbs over my nipples to send little spirals of pleasure down my spine. "I want to fuck you," he says simply.

"Tell me how you want it," I reply, almost dutifully. I never expected I would be like this in a sexual scenario: submissive and obedient. But with Konstantin, I never feel like he would ask me to do anything I don't already want to do. He knows what I like and what I need, instinctively, even if I don't say a single word.

"Turn around and bend over. Let me see that

beautiful ass," he orders, but even his demands are tinged with tenderness. I oblige happily, spinning around and leaning down to grab hold of the translucent safety bar. I cheekily sway my hips back and forth.

Konstantin's palm collides with my ass with a wet smack, the flash of delicious pain making me shiver. The Bull is usually surprisingly soft in bed, never pushing me too far. But sometimes, if I play my cards right, I can bring out a little more of the beast in him.

This morning shower is turning out to be my lucky day.

He rubs the head of his hard shaft against my ass while one of his hands slips down between my thighs, his fingers lightly stroking the length of my wet slit. I moan in anticipation, almost too afraid to move for fear that he might stop touching me. I crave his touch, his skilled fingers, sensual lips, and powerful cock, even when I'm asleep. So many nights I have fallen into fitful, sexually-frustrated dreams, only to awaken with the Bull himself beside me. All I have to do is kiss him awake, and from there we toss our clothes aside and fuck each other in the hazy morning light.

"You're so wet for me, *sakhar*," he growls, massaging my clit between his thumb and forefinger. The sensation is almost too intense, and my legs start to tremble slightly. Konstantin slaps my ass again, hard, making me cry out. He chuckles and slips one finger inside me, curling it into a come-hither motion to stroke expertly against my g-spot. His cock slides up and down against my ass as he finger-fucks me. I roll back into his touch wantonly, moaning and whimpering for him to finish me off.

"Tell me you want it," he orders quietly. "Beg for it, Rosie."

"Please, oh god, please let me come," I mumble, overcome with need. He slips a second finger inside of me, fucking me harder and faster while his other hand squeezes and smacks my ass, until finally I'm screaming, my honey gushing over his fingers. Before I even get a second to take a breath, he withdraws his fingers and pushes his cock inside of me instead, grasping at my hips and slamming into me again and again. The pleasure I'm feeling is so intense I can scarcely breathe, and it doesn't help that Konstantin is groaning my name over and over, like an epithet.

My second and third orgasms come crashing one after another, and by this point, the Bull nearly has to hold me up to keep me from collapsing. My legs are shaking and my mind is totally blank with all-consuming bliss, and just when I think I'm about to come down, a fourth climax shudders through my body and I squeal in spent delight. Konstantin thrusts into me more and more quickly, his control starting to wane, and finally he releases his seed deep inside me with a thunderous bellow.

Almost immediately, my head starts to feel fuzzy and the edges of my vision turn dark. My stomach lurches with nausea and distantly I can hear myself murmuring, "K-Konstantin," just before my legs give out and I collapse into darkness.

When I awaken, my head is still swimming, but now I'm lying on our bed instead of at the bottom of the shower. Konstantin is perched on the edge of the bed beside me, looking downright petrified with worry. I'm wrapped in a gigantic terry-cloth robe clearly meant for the Bull, and he's dabbing my forehead with a cool, damp washcloth.

"Rosalie?" he says softly, his voice piercing through the fog in my brain.

"Wh-what happened?" I whisper, my voice sounding thin and weak.

"You fainted, *moya lyubova*," he replies, stroking my cheek gently. My vision is starting to clear slightly now, and I can see that Konstantin has a towel wrapped around his waist, a sheen of sweat across his brow. He looks to have been suffering greatly while I was out.

"I don't feel so good," I manage to croak, trying and failing to sit up in bed. My head starts to spin and my stomach churns immediately. Konstantin delicately eases me back against the pillows again. He looks at me intently, and I can almost see the thoughts racing in his mind.

"Three days ago you said you felt ill, too," he says, thinking aloud.

I nod slightly, trying not to move too much.

"At first I thought maybe I was being too forceful with you," he reasons, and I can see the pain flicker across his face. I know the last thing he wants to do is hurt me.

"No, you're perfect," I assure him weakly. "There's got to be something else going on."

Suddenly, a flash of realization lights up his eyes and his jaw twitches. These are only subtle motions, but I know him well enough by now to spot his tell signs.

"*Oh bozhe*," he breathes, lifting one reverent hand to push the hair back from my face. "Rosie, *moya ptichka*, you might be pregnant."

The nausea in my stomach spikes and I groan, the real reason for my new physical weakness totally understood now. It makes sense. Of course I'm pregnant.

"But we... we have to be sure," I murmur. Konstantin nods and stands up.

"I will get you a test. And some ginger ale for your stomach," he says dutifully. "Will you be alright while I'm gone?"

"Mmm, sure," I reply, trying to keep my voice even. "I'll be fine. But… hurry back."

He disappears, leaving me alone with my thoughts for the next twenty minutes. What if he's right? What if I *am* pregnant? I don't have time for another baby — I am already taking care of Daisy and Sunny. I get another wave of dizziness at the thought of what will become of them once a new baby is in the mix. I can't do this. I can't build this new fairy tale life with Konstantin here, not while my little sisters struggle to even survive. It isn't fair to them.

What the hell am I going to do?

I'm still horribly conflicted when Konstantin returns. He unwraps the pregnancy test and helps me cautiously cross the room to the bathroom. A few minutes later, I stand with the little stick in my hand, staring in shock at the tiny plus sign.

It's true.

I'm pregnant.

I expected to feel anguish, total devastation and regret. But instead, it's like every terrible fear I had is now eclipsed by the overwhelming love I feel for the tiny life growing inside of me. I know, without a shred of doubt, that this is what I want. We will figure out the details somehow — saving my sisters, ending the slavers — everything.

When I tell Konstantin, his first reaction is to grin and throw his arms around me, pulling me close and kissing the top of my head. "I know you did not expect this, and neither did I. But Rosie, I am so happy. I never thought I could want something this much. But I do. I want to build a life with you, a family."

"Me, too," I mumble into his hard chest, soaking in his stability and warmth. He is my rock, my prince. The man who saved me from darkness and breathed new life into my lungs.

"I love you," he says, and I know he means it.

"I love you, too," I reply, feeling giddy with joy.

"But this… changes things," Konstantin continues, stroking my hair. "We need to expedite our plan, *lyubova*. I will make it happen. Do not worry about a thing."

I'm crouching behind a large billboard off the interstate, far north of the city. This place is out of my jurisdiction as *pakhan*. But then again, so is everything I'm ordering to be done today. This is the day I've been waiting for since my second day in New York, and it came so much sooner than I'd hoped.

"Begin," says the text message on my phone, and the moment I press a button to send it out, I know I've sealed the fates of nearly a dozen men. I have signed their death warrants.

The money Andrei and I acquired from our assassination and heist at the hotel a few weeks ago was not merely a vanity project to line our pockets. He and I both have deep purses, but to carry out what I've just ordered costs more than what a limitless credit card can buy.

While I've been training my lover, rebuilding the Bratva, and carrying out jobs in the area, Andrei and I have been assembling a list. We've dispensed of the formalities of keeping this business of rooting out the sex slavery trade within the Bratva, as we've long since realized that this corruption spreads farther than we'd ever imagined. My assassination of the politician on his own fishing boat made waves, but now, I mean to send a message louder and clearer than ever before, one that will silence the slave trade in Brighton Beach permanently.

Between our combined efforts, Andrei and I have a list of every major player left in the city who keeps the shamble of a sex trade alive. Some are Bratva. Some of them are politicians. Some are on the police force. And all of them must die. Every last dollar made from our heist at the hotel has gone towards carrying out the largest synchronized series of hits this city has seen in a very long time: everyone on our list is about to die within two minutes of each other.

That's why I took it upon myself to handle the most time-sensitive hit.

Coming over a hill on the interstate, I see the small motorcade that contains my target: Don Emilio Guarnieri, head of one of the largest Italian mafia families in New York. I went through my old politician target's files after his untimely death, and this is where the paper trail led me. The New York

Guarnieris have been tangentially profiting from the Russian slave trade for years, and since most of the Russians have gone underground, Don Emilio's profits have skyrocketed. What's more, if there's anyone who knows the root of the Russian connection, it's him and his capos. And they're all headed upstate for a weekend out.

I shoulder the rifle in my hand, looking through the scope and follow the cars carefully. It's overcast, with no chance of a glint off my scope's lenses. I couldn't ask for a better shot.

There are two cars accompanying Don Emilio's, one in front, one in back. A car full of men, I can deal with. The chance of my target escaping today, though, that's not something I'm willing to risk. So I level the crosshairs on the gas tank of the Don's sedan and take a slow, deep breath.

The sound of the shot is muffled by the blast of fire that envelops all three cars just after I pull the trigger.

The car in the back takes the brunt of the explosion, getting knocked upside down and rolling down into the ditch, its engine burning as the metal crumples around the unfortunate men inside. If any of them survived the first impact, the fire that engulfs the whole car a moment later finished the job.

Don Emilio's car was also thrown upside-down, and its burning remains now sit on the highway, and

I can see the terrified driver scrambling to get out, but the smoke obscures the Don.

The car in front was blasted forward, but it's still rolling, and it skids to a halt as I set down the rifle and start sprinting for the wreckage. I could waste shots trying to take all of them from the billboard on the ground, but as the smoke billows, it becomes clear that taking them on at close range would be more efficient.

I close the distance in a matter of moments, but I hear shouting in Italian, and gunshots are already ricocheting off the burning metal around me as I draw my pistol. I crouch behind the Don's car, and I hear the sound of footsteps coming around the corner to my left. I sweep the man off his feet with my leg, sending him tumbling to the ground before I take a quick shot to his head, ending him.

That gives away my position, so I dart in the opposite direction around the car, and a breeze tells me the smoke cover is about to dissipate temporarily. Bracing myself, I rise from my position and start firing, and the remaining guards duck and seek cover, but they find none as I pick the rest of them off one by one.

Suddenly, I feel a sharp pain in my leg as a man I hadn't seen following me kicks the back of my leg, sending me to my knee, hard. A hand with a knife in it comes around to cut my throat, but I grab his wrist, shifting back to hurl him over my shoulder and slam him to the ground in front of me. In an instant, I've wrenched the knife from his hand and driven it into his head from above.

As soon as the action started, it's over, and I hear coughing from Don Emilio's car. Slowly, I rise up, holding my pistol out and approaching the vehicle.

"Out of the car," I bark in Italian, "it's over, Don Emilio."

Sputtering, the aged man tears out of his seatbelt and crawls out of the overturned car. He starts to fumble for a pistol in his coat, but I kick it out of his hands, and he slumps against the charred metal of the car, a stream of blood running out of the corner of his mouth as he glares up at me, my pistol still trained on him.

"You," he manages, his breathing ragged. He and I both know he's burning through his last moments on this earth as he coughs up blood, despite his efforts to look dignified in this burning pile of trash. "I knew we never should have done business with the fucking potato farmers, no matter how sweet the Soviet cunts can be."

I fire my gun at the metal he leans on, and he recoils, terrified.

"Perhaps you didn't get the word about the change in management, Don Emilio," I growl, stepping closer to him. "The flesh trade is over. I'm shutting it down. You aren't the only target today." I start listing the names of those men who are dying even as I speak, but he waves indifferently, staring up at the cloudy sky.

"Dead men anyway. Diego, my right-hand man, he told me how he suspected you Russians' involvement in these assassinations around town. He said we should back out of the slave trade. He might have taken matters into his own hands if I'd continued to ignore him. Damn him, he was right."

"Women's lives are nothing more than money to you," I say, narrowing my eyes at him.

"Money and a good time," he tries to laugh, but he ends up coughing. "You won't get a repentance out of me in my last moments, you fucking snowbird. The Bull, they call you. Ha! You're getting goaded around by red capes, snorting and pawing the dirt."

"Speak clearly, *kozyol*! Anton! Where is he? He's the reason you're dying today, you owe him nothing."

The Don laughs, knowing he has something, anything over me, and I have to resist the impulse to put him down right this instant. "Right under your nose, idiot. But now? I think he'll be looking for greener pastures. Keep an eye on those who try to flee your ring, Bull. A fleeing coward is a deadly thing indeed. Maybe he'll give you one for me." He grins, his teeth stained with blood, and I raise my pistol to his head and put him out of his misery.

I stride away from the burning wreckage,

heading back to my sniping spot to gather my gear and disappear into the woods before the emergency servicemen arrive to clean up the mess. As I do, my phone lights up, and I put it to my ear.

"It's done," comes Andrei's voice, "the assassins have reported in. I assume you've succeeded?"

"Yes, comrade," I say, casting a rueful glance back to the street as I start marching into the wilderness, "but we can't rest easy yet. We have one more target to strike at, and it has to happen soon. Anton is still in Brighton Beach."

"And if it's at all possible, remember the E-N-G guideline. What's that again, ladies?" I ask, standing at the front of the room with my hands on my hips.

A chorus of six young women dressed in comfortable athletic wear, all rescued from the Bratva slavers, call out, "Eyes, nose, groin!" With each word, they simulate jabbing an imaginary foe in the eyes, punching him in the nose, and kneeing him in the crotch. I have to smile, I'm so proud of them. It's so fulfilling to be able to teach other women how to defend themselves, just like Konstantin taught me.

"Awesome job, everyone!" I declare, clapping my hands together. "Great work today! I'll be back on Thursday for our next session. If anyone has any questions, concerns, or if you just need someone to talk to, please don't hesitate to come to me, okay? I am here for you, every one of you."

The women all nod and murmur variations of *thank you* and *see you next time*. This is an abandoned warehouse on the outskirts of Jersey we've been using to meet up for therapy sessions, self-defense lessons, and just to congregate and get a sense of togetherness. I want more than anything for these women to know they're not alone, that there is strength in numbers, and even more strength in knowing your own worth. I am fully aware that my brush with the Bratva was nothing in comparison to what most of these girls have gone through.

One of them, a freckle-faced redhead named Valerie, was kidnapped from a shopping mall and sold to a horrible man who treated her terribly, keeping her as a maid and sex object. She was forced to clean his house and service him sexually for six months before Andrei and Konstantin found the man and eliminated him. Valerie is the most recent member of our group, and she's still understandably skittish. After what she's had to go through, I can't blame her for being paranoid and timid. She hardly ever speaks during our meet-ups, but I continue to encourage her to show up, because even if she doesn't really participate, at least our regular meet-ings lend some much-needed stability to her life.

I turn away to start packing up my belongings, getting out my cell phone to text Konstantin and let him know we are all about to head out. Just last month, he surprised me out of the blue with a brand new silver Fiat, stating that I need my own vehicle. He knows I don't really like to rely on him for everything, and he respects my independence. I like being able to drive around and enjoy my freedom. Especially now that I know how to take care of myself better than ever before. I'm stronger now, and I can look out for myself and my baby. And after all, it's still early enough in my pregnancy for me to safely teach these classes, at only four months. I'm physically feeling much better now that my nausea and dizziness are mostly under control, and I'm even starting to get that typical baby glow.

"Rosalie?" pipes up a meek voice from behind me. I turn around, surprised to see that Valerie is standing there fidgeting, her fiery amber hair hanging limply around her face. The poor girl has suffered immensely, still trying to regain the weight she lost during her six months of torture. She's only seventeen years old, and even though she's gone back home to live with her attentive parents, I think sometimes she still feels disconnected from her family. They will never really understand what happened to her or how to deal with it. Her trauma is unique to her own experience, and from what I have seen, a lot of families just don't know how to even approach such a terrifying event.

"Valerie, what is it?" I reply, careful not to step

too close. She still has huge issues with personal space and boundaries, and she shrinks away from even the slightest, most innocent touch. It's heartbreaking to see, but I like to think that she will get better with time and therapy. She's already a little more alive than she was when she first came to us.

"I-I just want someone to talk to, if that's okay," she murmurs, tucking her hair back behind her ear and blinking her big brown eyes sadly. She hardly looks her age; with her waifish frame and submissive stance, she looks more like a child. A lost child.

"Of course," I assure her, nodding. "Do you want to go somewhere more private to talk? Are you hungry? I can buy you lunch."

The faintest hint of a smile graces her face for a split second. "Y-Yes, that sounds good."

"Come on. You can tell me what's going on while we walk, okay?" I tell her.

I gesture for her to follow me, forcing myself not to try and embrace her, even though my nurturing instincts are dying to embrace her and comfort her like I would soothe a small child. But she is no ordinary girl, and the usual comforts won't help her. Valerie falls into step beside me as we walk out and get in my car to drive to a little roadside diner a couple miles down the road. I turn off the radio and glance across the console at her, waiting for her to begin.

Finally, she mumbles, "I'm s-scared that my family d-doesn't love me anymore."

My heart aches for her. I know how much it hurts to feel abandoned and out of place in your own household — years of neglect and outright violence from my father truly scarred me.

"Oh, sweetheart. Come on, you know that's not true," I try to reassure her.

"They treat me like some impostor or something. Like they want the real Valerie back, the old Valerie who wasn't afraid of things. But I don't know if I will ever be able to be her again. Not after what that monster did to me," she explains, her voice trembling.

"It just takes time," I say, but I know she doesn't believe me yet. It's too soon, too early in her recovery for her to be able to trust me or anyone else yet.

"I just don't understand how six months could change my whole life so much. I don't even feel like myself anymore, like the world is too big for me now. I try to sleep in my old bed at home but everything feels like it's the wrong size, wrong color. Sometimes I wonder if I even really exist or if I'm just imagining everything. Maybe this is all a dream and I'm going to wake up back in that cellar he made me sleep in."

"No, Valerie. This is your life now. This is the real world. You did it! You survived! The worst is over," I say vehemently. I want so badly to convince her everything is going to be better. I pull the car into the parking lot behind the diner and unbuckle my seatbelt. Valerie stares down into her lap, clearly trying to fight back tears.

"It's just… I feel like I'm not getting better fast enough," she admits, finally looking over at me, tears shining in her eyes. "I look around at everyone in our group, all those girls who are tough and confident and improving — and I feel so out of place. I don't fit in with them because I'm still broken. And I don't know if I will ever be whole again."

"You're still new to all this. It totally makes sense for you to be a little behind — it's nothing to worry about, I swear. Everyone feels like that at first, like they're never going to feel normal again. We're all good at hiding it, but I can promise you we all felt just the same way when we first got started. I still look at what happened to me and feel angry, hurt. It all depends on the day, too. You're going to have good days and bad days, but you can't let those negative thoughts and feelings define you, Valerie. Sometimes I still think about how much it hurts to know that my own father sold me away like I was nothing," I confess. "But you know what? I am better than that. I'm stronger now. I have a life of my own, and I'm making it work."

"I wish I had been sold to someone like Konstantin," she says quietly. "I can't imagine falling in love with my master. He was a horrible man."

"Konstantin didn't buy my love, Valerie. He saved me in the only way he knew how, and the rest… well, it just happened," I explain to her, shrugging. And it's true. There were times when I was suspicious of the Bull, thinking paranoid thoughts about how he probably just bought me like any other awful trafficker and then made up some story about saving me, to win my affection. But as I have come to know and understand him, I've realized how big a risk he's taking by doing everything he's done for me. After all, that first fateful night on the yacht, the guns were pointed at him *and* me. He had to do what he did. And I'm glad. Even if it means not getting to see my sisters… but we're concocting a plan for that, too.

"I just wish I had someone to love me and make me feel like a real person again," Valerie sighs, swiping at the tears in her eyes. "I want to be normal so bad, Rosie."

"I know. I understand. But changes come slowly, and you have to be prepared for the long haul. But whenever it feels like it's all too much, like recovery is too daunting, too impossible, just remember this: you survived the trauma. If you can do that, I know for a fact you can get through the recovery," I tell her firmly. She nods.

"Thank you so much for listening to me," she says, sniffling. "Thanks for everything."

"Don't mention it," I reply, smiling. "Now, let's go get some lunch. I'm eating for two and I'm starving!"

We spend the next hour or so chatting and sharing a pile of French fries and mini club sandwiches, talking about music and fashion. As it turns out, before she was kidnapped, Valerie was interested in pursuing a degree in clothing design. I encourage her to hold onto that dream, explaining that getting back into something she loved would probably help ground her and feel normal again. When we're finished eating, I pay the bill and drive her home, then I head off to the grocery store close to home for a few things.

As I'm walking back out to the car with two paper bags of groceries, I suddenly get the spine-tingling sense that someone is watching me, darting between the vehicles. I try to ignore it and carry on, chalking it up to some leftover paranoia from my years of living with Frank Barnes. I often have the feeling that something bad is about to happen, because for a large chunk of my life, bad things happened a lot.

But then as I approach my Fiat, someone jumps out behind me and tries to wrap an arm around my neck, holding a rag in their hand. I drop my bags and immediately jab my elbow back into my assailant's ribs, then swivel around and kick him in the groin. It's a lanky, dark-haired man with a thick mustache, and he's doubling over in pain. I spin on the ground and quickly dart for the car, my hands shaking as I start the engine. I back out of the parking spot and rush back home, dialing Konstantin's number on the way.

"*Ptichka*," his warm baritone voice says upon answering my call.

"Someone t-tried to k-kidnap me in the parking lot," I tell him urgently, tears burning in my eyes. "A man with a mustache. Tall and thin."

There's a long pause.

His voice instantly turns dark and somber when he replies, "Come straight home, *moya lyubova*. I will take care of this."

Going after me is a respectable thing to attempt. I have become a political figure, an issue of principle for the crime lords of New York City in my short time on American shores. To go after the love of my life is both cowardly and foolish. And I will make my enemies pay dearly for their mistake.

"The *mudak* is fleeing the city," I say as I storm down the hallway of the house as Rosie follows at my heels, and even the loyal guards who I've recruited to patrol the place look concerned by the stormclouds over me.

"Are you sure?" Rosie says, sounding more concerned that my information is accurate than anything else. She's taken her attempted abduction far better than I have. I'm ready to start ripping heads off up and down Brighton until I find the bastard Anton. "Have you heard back from the spies you sent to flush out the old safehouses?"

"*Da*," I say as I reach the room I've had converted into an armory, flicking the lights on to reveal the weaponry inside. My men have arranged my armaments ahead of time, at my demand. "And several small-time cravens have been dragged out of hiding, but I've got a tip from a reliable source. Remember Dmitri? I kept him on the inside; nobody near Anton knows we've been in communication. He says the rat is trying to slip out of town on that damned yacht."

Rosie's eyes darken. "*The Tsar's Palace?*" I nod, grimacing, then direct my attention to my weapons. I start strapping on guns and knives, even a grenade.

Glancing out the window at the night's darkness, Rosie chews her lip. "Won't he be gone already, then? He must have left before sunset."

"Very likely so," I say. "It's hard to sneak up on a boat in broad daylight, my love."

Her eyes widen. "You can't be serious."

"I've arranged a small rescue vessel I've had equipped for nighttime operations. I'll slip on to the ship and handle this personally. I don't know where Anton plans to flee to once he steps off that boat, but they'll be shipping his corpse instead." I consider strapping a bulletproof vest to myself, but it will only slow me down and be a risk around the black waters.

"You don't know how many people they have on

that ship," Rosie says anxiously, glancing at all the death devices I'm equipping myself with.

"I know."

"This could be a trap."

"I know."

"I don't want you to get hurt, Konstantin," she breathes, stepping in front of me and looking me in the eyes, and I look back at her long and hard before I nod.

"I know. But if that swine slips out of my grasp now, there will be many more women's lives to pay. A monster like that does not stop. He cannot stop. He *watched* as he made me take you, Rosie," I say, my voice a low growl as I put a gentle hand on the side of her face, brushing some of that gorgeous black hair aside. "A sadist like that must be put down. I should have killed him the moment he approached me."

Rosie takes a deep breath. She's grown so much in these past few months, and I couldn't be more proud. And truth be told, her precautions are more than just a lover's worry — this is the least preparation I've ever had for a job. But I'm still going to do it. It's a blind shot, but it's the only shot I've got. "I love you, Konstantin," she whispers, and I lean in, pressing my lips to hers, feeling the warm, soft moan she gives me in response as our bodies press together, my cock hardening at the very thought of coming back to her triumphant.

"Shining star of my life," I say into her ear, a thick husk, "I love you." We look into each other's eyes for a long, long time before I step away, striding out the door, and I can feel Rosie's eyes following me every step of the way.

* * *

THE LITTLE RESCUE boat has as quiet an engine as I can hope for as it blazes across the inky-black waters of the Coney Island Channel. I'm wearing all black. I should be outfitted in a wet suit and emergency diving gear, but I don't have time for proper professionalism.

Besides, this isn't just a professional matter. This is personal.

Up ahead of me, I can see the yacht leaving a broad wake, but its lights are off. The rat knows I've been keeping an eye out for him. Several eyes, in fact. I've had a network of spies reporting in hourly with the names of any Russians leaving or entering Brighton Beach, and the public transportation systems have been under constant surveillance. Anton knows I'm after him, and he knows he can't make it out by conventional means. If he cared about his lower-ranking soldiers, this ploy with the yacht might have succeeded.

I come within range of the ship, having been watching it with binoculars. I identify a good spot to board, and I ready the grappling hook gun I've brought with me. Once I'm on board, I have to move exceptionally quick. Anton probably didn't bring many guards on this job — too much movement would have alerted my spies. But those he must have brought will be an elite cadre of his most trusted men, and they will defend him to the death. Back in Russia, Anton was an affluent man. Here, he's proven just as dangerous and twice as illusive.

I aim the grappling hook at a corner of the boat and fire, and the hook sails through the salty air and finds purchase on the vessel. Testing the grip, I guide my boat closer to the side of the boat and secure the gun to my boat before shimmying up the unsteady rope, my gloved hands and thick boots giving me just enough traction.

The next moment, my feet hit the deck, and I look around me. Dead silence. Something feels wrong.

I draw a pistol and hold it at the ready, crouching and stalking forward. As I near the front of the deck, I squat by one of the columns supporting the upper deck and listen. There's nothing but the breeze and the sounds of waves lapping up against the ship. Strange that there are no guards outside, not even one.

Carefully, I make my way to the entrance to the ship's interior I was led through the night I was forced to claim Rosie. Gun at the ready, I push the door open, and it swings aside silently, the same old foyer sitting there, empty. And the door to the lounge where I fucked a woman — my *woman* — at gunpoint hangs open.

I can see nobody through it, so I put an ear to it, waiting. When silence greets me, I kick the door down and hold my gun out, tense and ready to strike.

Nothing.

I step inside, and the familiar sights fill me with such revulsion. Strange, considering how much joy the woman I met here has brought me, but I know not to give the feeling much credit. What Rosie and I cultivated together is something golden, eternal. What happened here was vile. We both know that, and tonight, I'm going to atone for it.

I was starting to suspect that this yacht was a dummy, an empty ploy to distract me while Anton made off by some other means, but this room feels...lived-in. I can't place why, but it seems like someone has used it recently. I step into the room, my eyes scanning around, but it's just the same old decadent, gaudy furnishing I remember.

Then my eyes fall to the table in the center of the room. My eyes linger on the ashtray in the middle of the room. A half-burned cigar sits in it. I step forward cautiously, moving around the side of the thing, and the smell of burnt tobacco hits me.

The sight of the faintest bit of smoke rising from

the still-glowing hot cigar greets me, and as I throw myself to the ground, I feel the bullet whiz past my left ear, missing me by fractions of a second before it hits the floor and ricochets out the window.

I turn and fire at the source, but I only see a blur of Diego Milani diving behind a couch as my bullets hit the wall behind him, and I push the heavy table over to give myself cover as well.

"You're a slippery man, Konstantin Alkaev," says Diego, calm and cocky even in the middle of the firefight. "When your friend Anton proposed this little date of ours, I'll be honest, I didn't think you'd show."

"What are you doing here, Diego?" I growl, my eyes scanning the room behind me for somewhere to move for advantage. To stay still is death. "This isn't your fight."

I hear him tutting, and it isn't muffled by cover. I stick my gun out and fire blindly, but I hear only his footsteps as he moves around the room. I stand up and aim, but I'm greeted by a bullet grazing my arm, and I curse as he gains cover under the bar at the far end of the room.

"You made it my fight, *Toro*." I fire at the liquor bottles above him, but the raining glass doesn't flush him out, so I retreat to the couch where he'd been a moment ago. "I don't like being toyed with, and that stunt you pulled with *la tua ragazza* in the hotel? That was a damn dirty move."

"So you help out a slaver for revenge?" I growl back.

"Vendetta is a complicated matter, my friend," he laughs, "It makes for strange bedmates. I was on the fence, but you mistreated Don Emilio so cruelly, I couldn't resist." He nearly purrs the last few words, and I know I'm dealing with the heart of a killer just as hardened as mine. "Don't worry, though," he adds candidly, "your bitch will be alright — I'll pay her a visit once your body is at the bottom of the sea."

Nearly seeing red, I pull out the grenade from my side and rip out the pin, tossing it through the air, and it clangs to the ground on the other side of the bar.

There's a pause before I hear "*Che cazzo?!*" as I'm sprinting out the door, and I round the corner to the stairs as I hear Diego scrambling after me. The grenade goes off before he can reach the door, and I waste no time in seeing if he made it out as I dash down the stairs to the lower decks.

I make my way down the long hallways until I reach a broad opening — the loading deck. It would have been here that Rosie was brought on board, I realize, but I don't have time to reflect on this, as I hear a voice down the hall.

"You're ballsy, I'll give you that," Diego snarls, and I hear his gunshots ring out as he fires experimentally down the hallway. "Fitting that you brought some explosives to play with. This ship is rigged with bombs, you could've blown us both up with that thing. But when I put a bullet in your fucking head, I'll set this whole ship ablaze, and the police will smear you as just some other fucking terrorist put to rest."

That's when an idea comes to me, and I pause, thinking a moment. Diego doesn't give me time, though, as I see him appear at the end of the hall, and we instantly raise our guns and fire at each other.

I see him nearly get knocked over as my shot hits his shoulder, but I feel a sting in my leg that tells me he landed one as well. *Fuck.* That's the last place I need an injury right now, but I'll suffer it. I turn and head through an opening to the engine room — the most effective place to situate a bomb in this situation, my old Spetsnaz training reminds me.

I can hear Diego's footsteps behind me as I hobble down the stairs, and inside, my eyes flit around the mess of exposed metalwork that chugs along, propelling us through the filthy waters. Diego wasn't lying. I can see explosives rigged up to a device at the far end of the room, and I race towards it.

As I suspected, it isn't active. Diego meant to set a timer after killing me and make his escape. Setting my hands on the console, I take a deep breath before I begin to tamper with a device, praying to the powers that be that time will be on my side.

Moments later, though, I hear Diego leap down

the stairs, and I hardly have time to move aside before his weapon fires, and I feel a bullet deep in my chest before I raise my gun to a standoff with him.

Both of us have blood streaming from our chests, and I wonder if my eyes are as bloodshot with fury as his. "Disarming the bomb ain't gonna help you, you fucking russky," he snarls, his breathing heavy. "You've thrown your life away trying to save some pricy cunts."

I smile. "Did Anton ever tell you why I was kicked out of the Spetsnaz, Diego?" He glares at me in response, so I continue. "I noticed some strange activity in my squad. Money changing hands. Men disappearing for the night in patterns. I did some digging. Turned out that our commanding officer was complicit in a sex ring. Can you imagine being one of those women — not only to have the law fail them, but to be held captive by the military's finest? It repulsed me. The *weakness* of my own comrades." I grip my chest as I feel a pang of pain shoot through it. "I killed them, Diego. I killed every one of the bastards. Military officials. So if you don't expect me to throw my life away for those women I didn't know..."

I step aside, revealing the ticking timer of the bomb behind me that I'd just rigged to go off in a few minutes. "...then I don't expect you to have figured out the lengths I'll go to protect the love of my life."

"Figlio di puttana!" he swears, firing his weapon at me as I dash towards him before he starts sprinting up the deck.

I've dropped my gun and drawn a knife from my side. I know I felt more beestings in my chest as his shots landed true, but I don't care anymore. Adrenaline is coursing through my body. Not even the pain in my leg can stop me. I'm going to end this. At any cost, including my life.

I chase the Italian through the corridors and towards the stairs with a limping gait. As he starts to mount them though, he turns around and tries to bring the butt of his pistol to my face. I catch him by the wrist and pull him down, slicing him across the chest as he falls.

He curses and kicks at my bad leg, sending me to one knee, and we grapple. I feel his hands around my neck, but I drive my knife into his side, and his grip slackens just enough for me to push him off me. I get to my feet and make for the stairs, but he tackles me, and I hit the stairs, turning over and trying to get his head between my thighs to choke him, but he's too quick, and I stand quickly, but not quickly enough to avoid a hard punch to the face that nearly dazes me. My hand goes out and grips his face, driving it hard into the wall behind him, then again, and again, and blood shows where I've struck him.

Finally, his grip slackens, and I let him crumple to the ground.

And I hear a blast from below deck.

My body turns as if forcing itself through a dream, and I see the opening of the deck above me, the dark night's sky just within my reach, and I just barely taste the salty air when fire consumes my world, and everything goes dark.

He looks so peaceful, lying on the hospital cot. His chest calmly rises and falls with strained breaths, his hard, handsome features softer than usual. He could almost be comfortably asleep, if not for the IV drip connected to his arm, and the bandages around his head, chest, and leg. I think back to the last time I heard his voice, confidently murmuring *I love you, Rosie*. Tears spring to my eyes as I wonder darkly whether he will ever wake up to say it again. There's so much I want to say to him, so many things I want us to do. But now I can only hope that his stormy gray eyes will open one more time. The doctors have been very attentive, and at my insistence, they have been keeping me in the loop more than I think they normally would.

It's been thirty-six hours since my phone rang and I received the terrible news: Konstantin was involved in an accident, and he's in critical condition. I had been sitting at home reading parenting books and trying not to think about the fact that the man I love was walking directly into danger. As the emergency room technician explained to me, Konstantin was fished out of the water after a massive explosion, the very yacht upon which we first met having sunken into the deep. The Bull has multiple injuries — two bullet wounds in his upper chest and left leg, second-degree burns down the right side of his torso, and a massive concussion which has left him more or less comatose.

As soon as the technician finished talking, my whole world started to spin. I dropped the phone and dashed for the bathroom to vomit, trying desperately not to pass out. I had to hold it together, for Konstantin's sake. And for our baby.

So I hurriedly jumped into the car and headed over to the hospital where Konstantin was being treated, tears blurring my vision as I drove. For the first several hours they would not let me see him, as he had been wheeled off to the emergency surgical unit to have the bullets removed from his flesh. And after that, they moved him to the burn unit, where he was under close surveillance for a few hours, as the doctors feared that his vulnerable, burned skin might have been exposed to some unpleasant microbes in the less-than-pristine water of the harbor. Luckily, he was not in the water for very long before he was discovered and rescued by an observant early morning fisherman, only moments before the cops and EMTs arrived.

His burns were not terribly severe, only affecting a strip of his torso down his right side, and because he was so quickly brought to the hospital, the doctors were able to clean and bandage his burns without any issues. A nurse in the burn unit reassured me that his skin would likely heal fairly quickly, with only a slight chance of scarring. Of course, I couldn't care less about the scarring — I just want him to wake up and be himself again.

But unfortunately, the force of the explosion hurled him about fifteen feet, causing him to hit his head on the hull of the yacht — hard. That is the blow that knocked him out and has kept him barely responsive ever since. Over this time, I have not left the hospital once, even to go home and shower. I've simply pulled my hair back into a messy bun and spent every minute by Konstantin's side, alternating between crying, talking softly to him, and dozing off only to wake up suddenly, in a frenzy. Even my subconscious mind won't let me rest, caught up in worrying about the man of my dreams and this living nightmare.

One of the nurses, a kind-eyed older woman called Hattie, has checked in on me periodically over the course of her thirty-six hour shift. She is always so gentle and upbeat when adjusting Konstantin's bandages and IV, making small talk with me about the baby and what our plans are for the future. As if nothing is wrong. Like Konstantin is just taking a long nap. At first, I was almost annoyed by Hattie's optimism, misinterpreting her aura as just not taking the situation seriously, thinking she was just trying to make light of Konstantin's injuries. But I understand now that she's doing this for my sake, to try and keep my spirits up. I know she's just trying to make me feel better and remind me that there is still hope, at least for us.

The Italian mobster who was on the boat with Konstantin has been in a similar state, a floor down from us in the same hospital. I will confess that when one of the younger, less experienced nurses accidentally let slip that the bastard was here, too, I was sorely tempted to go down there and smother him with a pillow or something. It's his fault Konstantin is lying in a hospital bed. It's his fault our life together, once so bright and full of promise, is collapsing around me now.

I clench my jaw bitterly, shaking my head as though to banish these grim thoughts. I know Konstantin wouldn't want me feeling this way toward anyone. He loves me for my gentleness, my compassion. But it's difficult to feel anything but sour hatred for that man a floor below us. I do take a miniscule amount of satisfaction in knowing that his own condition is worsening. He's in a far darker predicament than Konstantin, his prognosis severely stunted by his terrible injuries. From what I can tell, it is unlikely that he'll survive the night.

I'm not too broken up about that, to be honest.

But it does terrify me to know that the man dying downstairs went through essentially the same horrific experience that Konstantin did. They have similar injuries, even if the Italian man has it a little worse. I keep imagining that the same fate will befall the Bull — that he will die in a hospital bed, too. I will have to kiss my beautiful dream goodbye before it's even gotten a chance to really begin. I lean forward and rest my chin on Konstantin's right arm gently, careful not to put too much weight on it. In addition to the burns, gunshots, and concussion, his gorgeous body is marred with horrible bruises and lacerations caused by shrapnel from the explosion.

I look up at his serene expression, willing him desperately to wake up. To look at me and smile the way he used to. It still feels totally surreal, to see this man who is so powerful and strong, so full of life… reduced to a still, marble statue. But I refuse to think of him as empty just yet. The man I love is still in there, and even if the rest of the world eventually gives up on him, I will never stop waiting for his spark to ignite once more.

"Come back to me, baby," I murmur tearfully, lightly stroking his limp hand. "I miss you too much." There's nothing, not the slightest hint of response from his face or body. It breaks my heart to see him this way, but I have to be strong.

Finally, the urge to go to the bathroom overwhelms my desire to stay by his side, and I reluctantly tear myself away to go to the restroom down the hall from his hospital room. On my way back, I stretch my legs by walking over to the nurses' station to talk with Hattie. She looks up from her chart and gives me a cheerful, encouraging smile.

"Good to see you up and about, Miss Rosie," she chirps.

I nod. "Yeah. Apparently staring at him isn't going to wake him up any faster."

She clucks her tongue sympathetically. "It may not seem like it, but I know deep inside that pretty head of his, he knows you're there. He appreciates it, even if he can't show you that right now."

"I hope so," I reply, smiling half-heartedly. Out of the corner of my eye, I see a tall, olive-skinned man in a lab coat stroll into Konstantin's room. He looks a little taller than the doctor who's been checking in on us most frequently, but I chalk it up to my not thinking clearly at the moment.

I gesture down the hall toward him and say, "Oh, Dr. Duvall just went in there. I thought he wasn't coming back for another couple of hours. I hope nothing is wrong."

Hattie furrows her brows at me in confusion.

"Dr. Duvall is down in the surgical unit for the next few hours, assisting with an appendectomy."

"Then who just walked into...?" I trail off, my blood running cold.

Without wasting another second, I bolt down the hall to Konstantin's hospital room and fumble to throw the door open. It's locked.

"Hattie! Help! Somebody locked himself in there with my boyfriend! Help!" I scream, and she rushes over with a set of keys. "Come on, come on," I mumble, my heart pounding fiercely in my chest as she fiddles with the lock. Finally, the door pops open and I leap in front of the sweet old nurse so that she doesn't go in before me, unarmed and unsuspecting.

There's a man hovering over Konstantin's still body, a long, ominous syringe in his hand, aimed directly at a vein in the Bull's neck. The man looks up at me and I recognize him instantly. It's the man from the yacht. The one who sold me, who made us fuck at gunpoint.

Anton.

And now he's here trying to kill the man I love.

"Don't you dare touch him!" I scream, and to my horror he simply smiles. Hattie has come stumbling into the room behind me and Anton whips out a gun from a pocket in his white lab coat, aiming it over my shoulder at the nurse, who shrieks in fear.

"Get the hell out or I will shoot the old bitch," Anton snarls, cocking his gun.

"Oh my god," Hattie breathes, frozen in panic.

Anton uses the gun to gesture toward the door. "Or better yet, shut and lock that door. If anyone else comes in here, I will start shooting. But if you both behave, I'll give you front row seats to the execution of the Bull. What fun."

Hattie hesitates, and Anton shouts, "Do it now! Lock the damn door!"

She obeys and quickly returns to huddle behind me, trembling. Anton grins.

He turns back to Konstantin, preparing to prick him with the needle.

"Please, don't! I will give you anything you want. Whatever you want. Please, just don't hurt him!" I wail, stepping forward.

"Spoken like a true whore," Anton laughs. "But you know what I think? The only thing better than a live slut is a dead one." He holds up the gun, aiming it at my forehead.

Just as he is about to pull the trigger, there is a sudden rush of movement from behind him as Konstantin reaches out and grabs the villain's outstretched arm, causing the gun to go off, the bullet lodging itself in the wall. Anton cries out in anger and surprise, and before I can even think about Konstantin's miraculous awakening, I dive for the syringe, which has fallen to the floor in the struggle. Anton wraps his hands around Konstantin's throat and starts to squeeze. Konstantin is weakened from his injuries, and a feat he would normally be able to pull off with ease is too difficult for him now.

With Hattie screaming and cowering in the corner, Konstantin and Anton entangled in a battle of strength and will, I instinctively pick up the syringe and jab it into the side of Anton's neck. He shouts in agony and horror, immediately relinquishing his grasp and stumbling backward into the wall, yanking the needle out and tossing it aside, his eyes bugging out.

I rush to Konstantin's side, embracing him with hysterical sobs. Anton sinks slowly to the linoleum floor, his body giving out under the powerful toxin I injected into his bloodstream. Hattie flings the door open and bolts away just as a crowd of technicians and police come thundering into the room to secure the scene.

But everything happening around us is just background noise — the events unfolding in another world entirely, as nothing else matters but the two of us. Konstantin kisses me desperately, stroking my hair, my face, murmuring "I love you, I love you, I love you."

KONSTANTIN

To my advisors' chagrin, they've been unable to get me to dress like a *pakhan*. I can stomach the long meetings and constant calls, but I draw the line at thick, heavy suits with too much padding.

So it's in my usual gunmetal-gray suit that I fold my hands over one another as I sit at the end of a long, broad, mahogany table, the smell of smoke filling the air as the other leaders of the New York Bratva sit around, their eyes on me. When I speak, they listen. This is the respect I've seized in my time in America, and I will not let it go to waste.

Some of the men in attendance are emboldened by my presence, eager to comply with the changes me and so many like-minded men in our organization have striven for lately. Others look less at ease. I will deal with them in time.

"As for the stragglers, I can personally confirm," continues one of the leaders from the Brooklyn area, "that the last of the men who architected your arrival in Brighton as a bid for power have been dealt with, sir."

I nod to him, and he sits back down. "Let that be a message to our enemies. We, the Bratva, are united in our purpose, and the protection we extend will not be impeded by the ambitions of vermin." I have made it known that the names of the traitors are not to be spoken at these meetings, their names stricken from the annals of our society. It's a silly custom, but one that my new advisors suggested strongly, if only for a show of tradition.

"There are rumors," one of the leaders from Midtown speaks up, "that some of the accomplices who have helped our vision become a reality have fallen off the radar. I'd like to see these men duly rewarded for their service."

He speaks of Andrei, I know, as well as other skilled men who have been a part of this rather violent change in the status quo. "The men you speak of are under little obligation to reveal themselves," I respond, waving my hand to silence him. "But they will be honored nonetheless." I do not know whether the man who speaks does so out of genuine loyalty or a desire to root out men like Andrei, and the subtle glance I shoot one of my spies in the room tells him that finding this out is his next task.

"And what of the Italians?" says another higher-up, an older man who I know has deep ties outside the Bratva. "What do we make of them in light of their recent transgressions?"

"We must expect retaliation for the unfortunate death of Don Emilio," I say, standing up and striding around the room. "I do not know how deeply their entrenchment in the slave trade runs, but we must be cautious. If this is a matter we need to see to further, a light touch is preferable to open warfare with the mafia. I expect eyes and ears to be dispatched to Little Italy to answer that question."

"Pah!" comes a voice from the back of the room, "*Now* you preach caution? Where was that when you blew up a motorcade on the interstate to prove your point?"

A glare I cast across the room silences the man, and I let the pause linger in the room for a moment before I proceed. "There are times for peace and times for war," I say slowly, folding my hands behind my back. "There will be war if it is necessary, but there has been enough Russian blood spilled in the past months to merit caution."

The man gives a single, rueful nod of consent.

"But the reach of those who would carry on trafficking extends beyond New York," I continue, unfazed. "For this, an opportunity has presented itself. I've received word of motorcycle riders roving up and down the seaboard, a group of men and women based out of New Jersey, the sons and daughters of immigrants from the motherland. Reach out to these people, propose a friendship," I say with a gesture to those leaders of the southernmost reaches of the state, and they nod. "We will have more to discuss once these bridges have been built. I bid you all good day."

There's an exchange of farewells, and within a few minutes, the remaining men in the room are shuffling out of the room or talking amongst one another.

Before I leave, I take a moment to open a card that had arrived addressed to me. It was from a private investigator I hadn't deal with before, and had piqued my curiosity, but business had to be handled first.

What was inside surprised me, though.

His daughter has been found.

Simple. Straight forward. But there was only one person it must've been about, and I feel a sense of satisfaction that the man who helped me take out that slimy politician has found his lost daughter. It eases my mood, but as I head towards the exit, I'm followed by one of my spies. He catches up to me as I step into the evening air outside.

"My *pakhan*," he addresses me in a whisper, "I've

confirmed your suspicions of the smuggling ring upstate."

I nod, silencing him. He speaks of a concern I had regarding one of my alleged new allies who has been flirting with the Irish mob to resume activity under my nose in the city. Unfortunately for him, I pay my spies far better.

"Then you know what I would have you do, my friend," I say, clasping his shoulder momentarily without looking at him, and he nods. A moment later, he's walking away as if we've never spoken, as if I hadn't just ordered the deaths of several influential men.

But even as the weight of responsibility feels heavy on me, I feel it melting away as I see my Rosie waiting for me by the car down below, holding what looks like a couple of hot dogs for us to share.

"Looks like you had a fun meeting," she teases as a smile spreads across her lips, and I lean in to kiss her before accepting the food and raising an eyebrow at it.

"If we develop a taste for these things, we'll be dead before we can even start planning the wedding," I remark with a coy smile, and she giggles as I rub her swollen belly with my free hand.

"I think you've set a precedent for 'living a little,'" she remarks, holding up the massive diamond ring I gave her a week ago. I swear she still glows at the look of it as much as she did when I presented it to her.

"That's fair," I say, and we look into each other's eyes for a few moments before she blushes and looks away, stepping around to the car door.

"So, I'm getting to redesign the bedroom tomorrow, right?" she says, raising her eyebrows.

"For heaven's sakes, yes," I say, "And don't mind the expenses. Any price is worth it to improve that gaudy design."

"Don't worry," she says once we're inside the car, leaning over to kiss me on the cheek. "I'll spare no expense for my *pakhan*." I crack a smile and return her kiss, and we drive off to the place my new fiancé and I are quickly turning into a suitable place to call 'home.'

"What if they notice we're missing too long?" I giggle as Konstantin closes the door behind us. We're in the under-deck suite of our brand new yacht, with a group of our family and friends celebrating on the top deck.

The baby, a little girl we called Susanna after my mother, is six and a half months old, and the apple of everyone's eyes. Especially her young aunts, Daisy and Sunny. Soon after the incident at the hospital almost a year ago, Konstantin and I heard from our private investigator, Ilya, that my father had been arrested for gambling and prostitution once the string of assassinations brought attention to the sex slavery ring.

My sisters were about to be placed in separate foster homes when I showed up and immediately demanded that I be given exclusive rights to their guardianship. It didn't take much for the courts to agree, especially once it came to light that I spent the first eight years of their lives raising them virtually single-handedly. Ever since then, the girls have been living with Konstantin and me.

They warmed up to him slowly at first, suspicious of all men after their lifetime of neglect and abuse at the hands of our father. Plus, I think they still partially blamed Konstantin for taking me away from them. But it didn't take too long for him to win them over with his gentle affections. It certainly didn't hurt that he dotes on them like they're his own children. And once Susie was born, our family was complete. My eleven-year-old sisters, the new baby, the Bull, and me.

It's far from typical, but it's as close to perfection as I could ever imagine.

But there's only one thing missing from our beautiful family portrait — wedding rings. So now that the hubbub surrounding custody and crime has died down, Konstantin and I are planning an elaborate wedding and honeymoon in Europe. Which is why we bought this yacht: to sail around the ocean on a couple little weekend pre-marital voyages while we plan out all the details. Although I adore my three kids, I do miss having one-on-one time with Konstantin, and after everything we've been through, we're excited to finally relax a little and just enjoy each other's company. Of course, these voyages will be relatively tame and brief for now. After all, we do have a six-month-old baby. But luckily, we have a fantastic support group who are all jumping at the opportunity to fill out our little family.

Our friends Cassie and Andrei, along with a couple of the women from the self-defense classes and their boyfriends, are all babysitting the children right now on the top deck while Konstantin and I tour the bottom deck. And by "tour" I really mean "sneak away for some much-needed alone time."

"We'll be quick. And quiet," Konstantin says softly, giving me that devilish grin he's perfected just to talk me into things. But I playfully bat his shoulder.

"Be patient," I tell him, biting my lip. "We'll have plenty of time alone this weekend, remember? We can finally break in this new bed..." I saunter backward away from him and gesture elaborately toward the en suite bathroom. "...and this fancy shower. And we might just fuck on the top deck, too."

Konstantin chuckles and steps closer to sweep me into his arms, his once-stony face now brightened with true joy and contentment. I let out a surprised little squeal as he dips me backward, then swoops me back up to kiss me softly on the lips. I can't help but smile into the kiss, feeling safer and more loved than ever before.

Sometimes I still wake up expecting to find

myself back on that ratty futon at the house I shared with my family. My heart sinks and my stomach turns as I open my eyes, preparing to see the rundown house littered with empty booze bottles. But instead, I am greeted by the laughter of Daisy and Sunny, who often wake up before dawn to run around the house playing make believe, or by the sweet, plaintive wails of my baby girl. Or on rare, beautiful mornings, by the soft, rhythmic breathing of the beautiful man beside me.

Instead of seeing the decrepit shotgun house in Jersey, I awaken in the mansion, which has been sufficiently de-mafia-fied. With the help of Cassie, who has turned out to be a fantastic interior design assistant, we remodeled and redecorated the house from top to bottom. It now bears no trace of the hedonistic Bratva sin den it was before. Now it looks like a real home, with muted colors and homey touches. Konstantin and I had a fantastic time painting much of the house ourselves. It was messy, and it took us much longer than it would have taken a team of professionals, but it was fun. And that's what we're living for now — good memories.

As we walk up to the top deck, Daisy and Sunny come running over to throw their arms around Konstantin's waist, giggling excitedly. Cassie and Valerie are cooing over baby Susanna, while Andrei chats — albeit a little awkwardly — with Valerie's boyfriend. Little Max toddles around making whooshing noises as he holds a tiny toy airplane above his head. My heart feels full to bursting as I look around at the beautiful family I've found.

Of course, there are times when I look back on bad things that have happened to me, and occasionally I still feel a pang of bitterness, wondering why me? And then, I look around at all the happiness surrounding me and it all starts to make sense.

Maybe all those years of suffering comprised a test of fate, to see if I would give up or keep going. And even when my life became so daunting, so overwhelmingly hard that I felt crushed by the weight of my responsibilities and fears — I pressed on. I passed the test, and now I'm collecting my reward.

I am determined to spend the rest of my life making so many wonderful memories that I can scarcely remember the bad ones anymore. I want my head to be so filled with light that there's no room left for darkness. Konstantin has a shadowy past, as well, and he understands me better than anyone else when I say that I refuse to let my yesterdays define my todays.

And I damn sure won't let anything stand in the way of a bright, shining tomorrow.

THANK you so much for reading! I hope you enjoyed

<3 If you have a moment, please leave a review. Other readers are dying to know what you thought.

I have plenty more bad boy romance for you, including the rest of the Hitman Series, so make sure you check out my other books on the next couple of pages, and sign up for my newsletter to be notified when I have a new release on the way!

Owned by the Hitman
Ebook | Audiobook | Paperback

Sold to the Hitman
Ebook | Audiobook | Paperback

Saved by the Hitman
Ebook | Paperback

Captive of the Hitman
Ebook | Paperback

Stolen from the Hitman
Ebook | Paperback

Hostage of the Hitman
Ebook | Paperback

Taken by the Hitman
Ebook | Paperback

GLOSSARY

RUSSIAN

- *pakhan* : the leader of an area's Bratva presence, similar to a Godfather
- *boekiv* : literally 'warrior,' the rank of a made man in the Bratva
- *zvyovdochka* : little star
- *kozyol* : goat, used as a male-specific insult
- *mudak* : asshole

ITALIAN

- *toro* : bull
- *la tua ragazza* : your girl

- *che cazzo* : what the fuck
- *figlio di puttana* : son of a bitch

Killing For Her

Abducted

STEPBROTHERS:

Ruthless

Criminal

STANDALONES:

Betting on Love

Hunter's Baby

I Hired A Hitman

Vegas Boss

Rock Hard Bodyguard

Innocence For Sale: Jane

Redeeming Viktor

<u>Romance:</u>

Falling for her Boss (Novella)

Most Wanted: Lilly (Novella)

Bound as the World Burns (SFF)

<u>Erotic Thriller:</u>

THE **D**ANGEROUS **M**EN **S**ERIES:

The Narrow Path

Strayed from the Path

Path to Ruin

ABOUT THE AUTHOR

Alexis Abbott is a Wall Street Journal & USA Today bestselling author who writes about bad boys protecting their girls! Pick up her books today if you can't resist a bad boy who is a good man, and find yourself transported with super steamy sex, gritty suspense, and lots of romance.

She lives in beautiful St. John's, NL, Canada with her amazing husband.

facebook.com/abbottauthor

twitter.com/abbottauthor

instagram.com/alexisabbottauthor

bookbub.com/authors/alexis-abbott

pinterest.com/badboyromance

youtube.com/AlexisAbbott

ACKNOWLEDGMENTS

Thank you to my amazing Patrons. I'm constantly humbled and grateful for your support.

Ramona Cabrera
Melissa Hedrick
Virginia Swanson
Dawn Daughenbaugh
Don Doss
Stacie Currie

If you'd like to join them — and get my ebooks or paperbacks — you can find me here on Patreon.
https://www.patreon.com/alexisabbott